Courteous, courageous and commanding—these heroes lay it all on the line for the people they love in more than fifty stories about loyalty, bravery and romance.
Don't miss a single one!

AVAILABLE FEBRUARY 2010

A Vow to Love by Sherryl Woods
Serious Risks by Rachel Lee
Who Do You Love? by Maggie Shayne and Marilyn Pappano
Dear Maggie by Brenda Novak
A Randall Returns by Judy Christenberry
Informed Risk by Robyn Carr
Five-Alarm Affair by Marie Ferrarella

AVAILABLE MARCH 2010

The Man from Texas by Rebecca York
Mistaken Identity by Merline Lovelace
Bad Moon Rising by Kathleen Eagle
Moriah's Mutiny by Elizabeth Bevarly
Have Gown, Need Groom by Rita Herron
Heart of the Tiger by Lindsay McKenna

AVAILABLE APRIL 2010

Landry's Law by Kelsey Roberts
Love at First Sight by B.J. Daniels
The Sheriff of Shelter Valley by Tara Taylor Quinn
A Match for Celia by Gina Wilkins
That's Our Baby! by Pamela Browning
Baby, Our Baby! by Patricia Thayer

AVAILABLE MAY 2010

Special Assignment: Baby by Debra Webb
My Baby, My Love by Dani Sinclair
The Sheriff's Proposal by Karen Rose Smith
The Marriage Conspiracy by Christine Rimmer
The Woman for Dusty Conrad by Tori Carrington
The White Night by Stella Bagwell
Code Name: Prince by Valerie Parv

AVAILABLE JUNE 2010

Same Place, Same Time by C.J. Carmichael
One Last Chance by Justine Davis
By Leaps and Bounds by Jacqueline Diamond
Too Many Brothers by Roz Denny Fox
Secretly Married by Allison Leigh
Strangers When We Meet by Rebecca Winters

AVAILABLE JULY 2010

Babe in the Woods by Caroline Burnes
Serving Up Trouble by Jill Shalvis
Deputy Daddy by Carla Cassidy
The Major and the Librarian by Nikki Benjamin
A Family Man by Mindy Neff
The President's Daughter by Annette Broadrick
Return to Tomorrow by Marisa Carroll

AVAILABLE AUGUST 2010

Remember My Touch by Gayle Wilson
Return of the Lawman by Lisa Childs
If You Don't Know by Now by Teresa Southwick
Surprise Inheritance by Charlotte Douglas
Snowbound Bride by Cathy Gillen Thacker
The Good Daughter by Jean Brashear

AVAILABLE SEPTEMBER 2010

The Hero's Son by Amanda Stevens
Secret Witness by Jessica Andersen
On Pins and Needles by Victoria Pade
Daddy in Dress Blues by Cathie Linz
AKA: Marriage by Jule McBride
Pregnant and Protected by Lilian Darcy

TERESA SOUTHWICK

IF YOU DON'T KNOW BY NOW

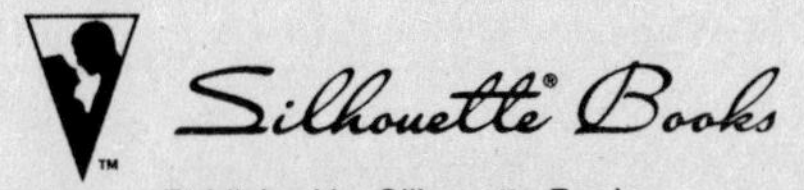

Published by Silhouette Books
America's Publisher of Contemporary Romance

Recycling programs for this product may not exist in your area.

ISBN-13: 978-0-373-36288-2

IF YOU DON'T KNOW BY NOW

This edition published by arrangement with Harlequin Books S.A.

For questions and comments about the quality of this book please contact us at Customer_eCare@Harlequin.ca.

Visit Silhouette Books at www.eHarlequin.com

Printed in U.S.A.

TERESA SOUTHWICK

lives with her husband in Las Vegas, the city that reinvents itself every day. An avid fan of romance novels, she is delighted to be living out her dream of writing for Silhouette Books.

Chapter 1

Maggie Benson's jaw dropped.

She stared at the man standing five feet away and wanted to pinch herself—or him. Was she dreaming or hallucinating? Any second she expected to hear a rousing rendition of the *Twilight Zone* theme. The guy standing just outside her rodeo booth was the spitting image of Jack Riley. But that couldn't be. They said everyone had a double, this must be his. Jack was a love-'em-and-leave-'em rogue she'd never expected to see again.

"Hello."

Now she was hearing things. One word, and she knew his deep, gravel-roughened voice.

"Jack?"

"Yeah, Maggie."

It *was* him. God help her—Jack Riley had returned. And she didn't know whether to hug him or hit him.

Trembling started in her hands and spread to her legs, turning them the consistency of crème brûlée, the soft part just below the crunchy, crystallized top. As if that wasn't bad enough, her heart pounded almost painfully. Then her palms began to sweat, making a friendly handshake out of the question. But then, considering what they'd done ten years ago, shaking hands with sweaty palms was small potatoes.

The man standing close enough to reach out and touch had been her first time, something a girl never, ever, forgot. But she couldn't say the same for him. He'd walked away and never looked back.

And, damn him, he was still so bad-boy handsome he trapped the breath in her lungs until her chest was near to bursting. Eyes as deep and blue as a field of Texas bluebonnets and fringed by incredibly thick, sooty lashes looked her up and down. He had the same black hair cut conservatively short—military short, she noted with a catch in her heart.

She hadn't seen him since he'd left Destiny hardly more than a boy. It was ten years later and he was back—bigger, broader, built.

Jack Riley was a man.

"It's good to see you, Maggie," he said as she continued to stare.

How could he just disappear for ten years, then show up without warning at the North Texas High School Rodeo Championships? What was she supposed to say?

"Cat got your tongue?" he asked as if he could read her thoughts.

She shrugged, shook her head and extended her hands

palms up in a completely helpless gesture. After all that, the best she could come up with was, "Wow."

"That's a start."

He studied her with eyes that looked as if they had seen too much, as if they could laser all the way to her soul. If there was a God in heaven or any justice in the world, he wouldn't be able to see her secret. Not now. Not yet.

"How've you been?" she asked.

"Fine. You?"

"Great." Could this be more awkward?

"You look like you've seen a ghost."

"Probably because I feel that way." She brushed her hands down the sides of her jeans and took a deep breath. "Earlier, I thought I saw you. I mentioned it to Taylor Stevens, but I figured I must have been mistaken. Ever since, I've had this weird, déjà vu-ish kind of feeling."

"It was me."

"Why didn't you come over then?"

Instead of answering he picked up one of her business cards in the holder on the ledge of her booth. "This 'N That? Maggie Benson, owner?"

"It's my shop. I opened it in downtown Destiny five years ago."

"What kind of shop?"

"Collectibles, antiques, crafts. Souvenirs, shirts, hats, beaded purses. I'm in charge of selling the official T-shirt for the North Texas High School Rodeo Championships." She picked one up and unfolded it, displaying the back for him. Why did her hands have to shake so? "See? All the kids' names are on the back. I also personally embroider and paint jackets and T-shirts," she said, indicating the samples hanging from the wooden walls of the booth.

She opened her mouth to say more, then caught the inside of her top lip between her teeth. Drastic situations called for severe measures. She really did need to stop babbling. It wasn't her job to fill awkward silences. He'd turned his back on her. Let him do the talking.

"Impressive," he commented, gazing at the scene on the back of a jacket, as well as the other goods arrayed on the wooden walls.

"Thanks." She met his gaze, determined to see his one-word answer and *not* raise him.

He leaned a broad shoulder against the corner two-by-four holding up her booth. "Surprised to see me?" he finally asked.

Try shocked. Add dumbfounded, amazed, astonished, disconcerted, then toss in a healthy dose of confusion and that might just about describe what she was feeling. A little surprised? Apparently sometime during the past decade he'd taken a crash course in the finer points of understatement. He might have thrown her for a loop, but wild horses couldn't drag the nerves out of her—in spite of the fact that they were bucking through her like a spooked stallion.

Casually, she rested a hip against the wooden ledge mere inches from where he lounged. "Why would I be surprised to see you? You went to boot camp. We exchanged some letters. You disappeared without a trace." She shrugged, struggling for nonchalance, but very afraid she'd failed miserably. "Happens all the time."

"I'm not much of a letter writer."

"Really? Your last one was pretty straightforward. You dumped me."

Along with a girl's first love, she never forgot the details of her first broken heart. Maggie'd wadded up the one sheet of paper and tossed it into the trash, but certain phrases were forever branded on her mind.

Getting too serious. Not fair to you. Best to go our separate ways.

But she didn't say any of that. It was ancient history. "If I remember correctly, you said your life was too unstable for a relationship with anyone."

"Yeah." His gaze slid away and he stared off into the darkness over her right shoulder. A muscle in his lean cheek contracted as his lips thinned into a straight line.

"I sent one more letter after that. It came back with Return to Sender in your handwriting. Not a single word from you since. Now here you are." She lifted one shoulder in what she hoped was a carefree, unconcerned gesture.

But she was very concerned. Her returned, unopened letter had come as a shock, followed quickly by panic and unbelievable pain. She'd been a scared teenager with a small problem that would get bigger by the month—not to mention raging hormones and a romantic streak a mile wide. She'd thought she loved him and would never stop. But she wasn't a teenager any longer. Circumstances had forced her to grow up fast. And her romantic streak had been pounded, if not into submission, at least into realistic expectation based on past experience.

She'd learned that love *did* stop.

"I shipped out right after boot camp," he said, then raised those broad, mouth-watering shoulders as if that explained everything.

"No need to apologize," she said.

"That was an explanation."

"Okay. But I'm not mad."

"Oh?" The ghost of a smile flirted with the corners of his mouth.

She tossed her head in a careless gesture that swung her red curls around her face. "Don't be silly. I'll admit I was miffed for a while, but I got over it. Years ago. My life is together. I'm all grown up."

"So I see," he said.

His lips curved up then, turning the dimples in his cheeks into vertical lines on either side of his mouth. A look glittered in those blue eyes that started a quivering inside her the likes of which she hadn't experienced in a decade. Damn it. Ten lousy years and no man had done this to her. Five minutes with Jack Riley and she was practically a puddle of goo at his feet. Still, she hung on to her composure as if it was the last handhold between her and a five-hundred-foot drop.

She folded her arms over her breasts, just in case her white T-shirt and bra didn't hide the way her nipples stood at attention and saluted the fact that Jack Riley was back.

"So what have you been up to all these years?" she asked, putting just the right amount of chatty interest in her tone.

His face darkened, then went blank. It was as if he'd stepped beyond the light and back into the shadows. If he hadn't just nearly cracked a smile, she probably wouldn't have noticed the withdrawal. But he did and she had.

He looked at her card, still in his hand. "This and that," he said.

Well, wasn't he just a regular gusher of information, she thought. "When did you get into town?"

"Today."

"What brought you back?"

"Personal business."

"Oh?"

"And a newspaper story."

She didn't remember ever having to yank information from him like an impacted wisdom tooth. But then, when they'd managed to steal time together, talking hadn't been tops on the To Do list.

The memories churned up by that thought brought heat flaring into her cheeks. Sneaking around to meet him. The feel of his strong arms tightly wrapped around her. Kissing as if she couldn't get enough. It had been exciting, thrilling.

She lifted her chin slightly, to study him better. She hadn't known him very well when he'd left, and she certainly didn't know him now. If twenty questions was the way he wanted to play, she was just the gal for it. Because she had more than twenty questions she wanted to ask him.

"What story was that?" she asked.

"An article in a syndicated newspaper advertising the dates of the high school rodeo championships along with info about the new dude ranch Taylor Stevens is opening. There was a picture, too, of Mitch Rafferty and Dev Hart with Taylor."

"I'm impressed."

"Hmm?"

"That was a whole bunch of words strung together. Two whole sentences if I'm not mistaken. Compound sentences. Be still my heart."

He tucked her business card into his shirt pocket. "Military training."

"What about it?"

"Takes all the fun out of—" He stopped, his gaze dropping as if he'd revealed too much. Then all he added was, "Communication."

"I guess I'd never make it in the military. Too communicative."

"Magpie," he said.

That one word wasn't enough to tell her if he was being thoughtful, wistful or just plain sad. His expression was wiped clean of emotion. What was he thinking? Feeling? *Anything?* The Jack she'd known had been easy to read—once she'd gotten past his rebellious, bad-boy facade to find the gentle, caring teddy bear underneath. That guy had worn his heart on his sleeve, as much as any teenager could. She'd been able to read him easily. But they hadn't connected until the last couple of weeks in his senior year, after he'd already signed his recruitment contract.

If he hadn't gone into the army, what would have happened? she wondered. Would they be together now? Or would some tart have stolen his heart? Her stirring memories of his not-very-well-concealed emotions swung the floodgates of her curiosity all the way open.

"So, tell me what you've been up to," she repeated casually.

"I travel a lot. I'm never in one place very long."

"Why?"

For the second time he ignored a direct question. But this time he grinned, his first genuine no-holds-barred smile. The effect was enough to knock Maggie on her backside and she couldn't make herself care that he hadn't answered her. If there'd been a spotlight on his mouth at that precise moment, the resulting brillisant glare off his straight, white teeth would have folks blinking their eyes and reaching for their sunglasses. God help her, she was reaching for her heart and hanging on to it with both hands.

"What?" she asked as he continued to look at her.

"Just the same straight-talking Maggie."

Not quite the same, she thought.

"So you're never in one place for long? The military?" she guessed, and his nod confirmed it. "Do you miss your dad?"

"Not much. Not anymore."

His father had passed away five years ago. A heart attack. She'd heard Jack had come back to help his grandmother handle the details. But Maggie had been out of town, on vacation with her folks in Florida. She hadn't seen him and had been relieved and sorry in equal parts. She'd chalked it up to destiny.

Suddenly a thought struck her about the "personal business" he'd returned for this time. And she realized that, for a while, a part of her had always expected him to show up. When he hadn't, she'd let it go. Which was why seeing him tonight had come as such a shock.

"I'm sorry about your grandmother. We missed you at the funeral. More than half the town came. I'm sorry you couldn't make it."

Another shadow crossed his face. "Me, too."

"Why weren't you there?"

"I was…working."

The slight hesitation and pain in his voice told her a lot. "Dottie said she didn't hear from you much.

That personal messages don't get through when you're involved in a project."

"Yeah."

"But she died six months ago. That's a pretty long time. What kept you?"

He lifted one shoulder. "I missed the funeral. After that, it didn't matter when I got back."

"Some job. Dottie also said that it sucked you in like a black hole."

"Gran had a way with words," he said sadly.

"She loved you, too. And was very proud of the fact that you serve your country. I was very fond of her."

Five years ago she'd opened her shop and moved out of her parents' home into an apartment. Three and a half years later she'd found her very own affordable house right next door to Jack's grandmother's. For a year and a half Dottie Riley's home-baked cookies, pies and zucchini bread—not to mention friendship and wisdom—had been very precious to Maggie.

The older woman had always gone to great lengths to make sure Maggie had known that Jack wasn't involved in a relationship. She'd taken a certain satisfaction in that. Maggie had adored her. So had Faith.

Her daughter. And his. Maggie had tried to tell him and would have if he hadn't disappeared. She'd eventually decided it was best to not say anything. Although she probably should tell him now. But it wasn't something she could just blurt out. Besides, based on past history, he probably wasn't planning to stay in Destiny. He would take care of Dottie's estate, then head out. This time for good since he had no family here.

Correction: no family that he knew about.

Her gaze scanned the rodeo crowd in search of her

daughter's curly black hair. A while ago Faith had been in the stands with Sheriff Grady O'Connor, his twin girls and Jensen Stevens. Looking in the same place where she'd last seen them, Maggie spotted the sheriff, but everyone else was gone.

"Where'd they go?" she muttered, craning her neck.

"Who?" he asked, half turning to see where she was looking.

"The three little girls I'm keeping my eye on," she said vaguely. "They've been flitting around those stands like bees looking for pollen."

"What do they look like?" he asked.

Maggie wanted to say, "One has your eyes and hair color, combined with my curls." Fortunately good sense prevailed.

"Two are identical—Grady's twins. The other one is wearing blue jeans and a neon-pink T-shirt."

He scanned the bleachers. Maggie had the feeling that his scrutiny was methodical and relentless, as if he were stalking his prey through a pair of binoculars. She shivered at the thought. There was an alert intensity about him that she didn't remember. She wondered what had happened to him in the years since she'd last seen him.

"Nothing."

"Me, either. Darn it. Just a while ago, a man approached them. A stranger."

"It's championships," he said. "There's bound to be people you don't recognize."

"I know. But this guy just gave me a bad feeling. Go ahead and laugh."

He shook his head. "I've learned to never underestimate gut instinct."

"Okay."

How had he learned? She was curious but wouldn't ask any more than she would explain the odd sensations she'd had all night—after catching a glimpse of him. When Taylor Stevens had stopped by her booth, Maggie had shared the fact that she was creeped out. That ever since Mitch Rafferty had returned to Destiny, it was as if the past was catching up with all of them.

She'd teased that he was a cosmic catalyst, and wasn't so sure that it wasn't the truth. Just then the sheriff had joined the girls and the stranger had disappeared. Now that she couldn't see the girls, Maggie's bad feeling kicked up again, this time into overdrive.

At that moment she spotted Taylor's sister, Jensen, strolling by the booth. "Jen?"

The stunning green-eyed brunette stopped and looked. "Hi, Maggie." She walked over to the booth. "You look familiar," she said to Jack.

"Jack Riley," he said.

"Now I remember." She slid Maggie a look that said she approved of her taste in men. Then Jensen looked more closely and asked, "What's wrong, Maggie?"

"I saw you in the stands with the girls a little while ago, Jen. Did you see which way they went?"

She nodded. "I think Kasey and Stacey were on their way to the refreshment stand. Faith was headed in the direction of the stock pen."

"Doggone it. That girl doesn't have the good sense God gave a grasshopper." She met Jack's intense gaze and tried to tamp down her reaction. The last thing she wanted was him questioning anything until she had a chance to think this through.

"I'm sure Faith is fine," Jensen assured her.

"Do me a favor, Jen? Watch my booth while I see what's what?" Maggie opened the wooden door as she spoke.

"Sure," the other woman answered, changing places with her. "I'll do the best I can to hold down the fort."

"Don't worry. It was busy before the rodeo events started but now it's slow. Intermission is almost over so you shouldn't have a problem. I'll be back in a few. Thanks, Jen. 'Bye, Jack," she said, starting off in the direction of the stock pen.

"I'll go with you." He fell into step beside her.

"That's not necessary," she answered, hurrying to keep up with his long-legged stride.

It briefly crossed her mind to sprint away. But he had her on height, six foot one to her five foot two. And with those thick ropy thigh muscles rippling beneath his denim jeans, she didn't have a prayer of outrunning him. Besides, he would wonder why and probably ask. And she couldn't give him an answer.

When they reached the stock pen, the smell of hay and dust was strong. In spite of the haze kicked up by the animals, she had no trouble spotting Faith at the far end of the enclosure. True to form, the girl was perched precariously on the top rung of the fence, watching the activity. She faced outward, her bottom hanging over the slat, on the animal's side. Maggie's bad feeling just got worse.

"Faith," she called when they were a few feet away. "Get down from there."

The little girl saw her and started to wave, using her whole body to do it. "Hi—"

The next thing Maggie knew, her child had lost her balance and was tumbling backward into the wooden steer enclosure. Everyone's attention was on rodeo commissioner Mitch Rafferty, standing with a microphone in the center ring. Nobody close to Faith had noticed her fall.

"Oh, God—" Maggie's heart leaped into her throat. She felt as if she were trapped in a nightmare, trying to wade through hip-deep honey to get to her daughter.

But Jack didn't hesitate. Without a word he jumped onto the middle rung of the fence, then swung himself over and into the pen. He slapped the rumps of the milling steers to move them out of the way. In the next instant he scooped Faith up into his arms and turned his back, putting his body between the little girl and the nervous animals tossing their wide heads with the dangerous horns. Seconds later he climbed back over the fence, still holding the child.

With her arm around his strong neck, Faith smiled at Jack. "Thanks, mister."

"You okay?" he asked.

"Yeah." Then Faith spotted her. "Maybe not. But it's okay if you put me down now. It's time for me to suffer dire consequences."

"Are you hurt?" Maggie took her daughter by her upper arms and checked her freckled face for bumps and bruises. Fortunately, she didn't find any. There were red spots on her pink shirt, but that was a cherry snowcone stain. The worst of the ordeal seemed to be the muck and straw mixed with dust that stuck to the backside of her britches.

"She's okay." Jack scanned the crowd. "But I think we should find her folks."

Faith's blue-eyed gaze—Jack's eyes—swung from Maggie back to him. "You can stop looking for my folks," the child said.

"What?" he asked, sounding puzzled.

"It's just Mom and she's right here."

Maggie flinched and glanced all the way up at him. His face was still carefully blank, but he tensed, as if every cell and nerve in his body had gone on high alert. She noted a vague feeling of satisfaction that she'd finally been able to detect any reaction at all in him. Unfortunately her hope that he would have no comment was swiftly shattered.

"'Mom'?" he asked, raising one eyebrow.

Chapter 2

Maggie had a kid? A little girl.

Jack wasn't sure why that surprised him, but it did. He'd thought about her over the years. Visions of her red curls and hazel eyes had crept into his mind at the weirdest times. Not to mention her sweet, lush lips that had done things to him he would never forget.

But he wasn't a dope. She'd hardly been more than a girl when he'd left. He'd known she would grow up, and grow up *fine,* but he'd never pictured her with a kid.

"This is my daughter, Faith," she said, hesitating slightly.

Most people wouldn't have noticed that she missed a beat. But he wasn't most people. He was a career soldier whose life and the lives of his men depended on him noticing even the slightest twitch. He was the computer expert, a military operative in the field who got the job done. So he noticed that Maggie was nervous and trying to hide it.

"Sweetie," she said to the girl, "this is Jack Riley—G.G. Dot's grandson. He's an old friend of mine."

"He doesn't look old," the little girl commented, glancing shyly at him.

Maggie slid him a slightly uncomfortable look. "I meant that I've known him for a long time."

"Then how come I never met him before?"

"I've been gone," Jack said. In more ways than one, he thought. G.G. Dot? Must be some nickname she'd come up with for Gran. "Hi, Faith. Nice to meet you." He held out his hand.

The child put her smaller one in his. "Nice to meet you. Why did you go away?"

"Sweetie, it's not polite to ask questions."

Since when? A few minutes ago Maggie had asked whatever popped into her mind. Grilled him like a raw hamburger. If he had a dollar for every time she'd said the word why, he would be on his way to financial security. He studied the two—the kid's hair and eyes were different. But she had Maggie's stubborn, confident stance. And curiosity. She was definitely a Maggie in the making. Like mother, like daughter.

Faith's beautifully shaped little mouth puckered in a familiar pout. It looked suspiciously like an expression he remembered from her mother, a decade ago.

"How am I s'posed to get to know him if I don't ask questions?" the kid asked.

"She has a point," he said to Maggie. Although he wondered if he should tell the girl that when she actually got to know him, she wouldn't like what she found. Nah. He wouldn't be here that long. What could it hurt to let her keep looking at him as if he were a hero? "I joined the army," he explained. "I'm on leave." When she turned a puzzled frown on him, he added, "It's like vacation."

"Do you hafta go back?"

"Yes."

For some reason he felt compelled to answer her questions. Was it those big blue eyes looking at him as if he was ten feet tall? Or was it something about being back in Destiny? Something that brought out memories he'd tried to forget.

Like Maggie. And the way she'd felt in his arms with her mouth soft against his.

"So you're officially still in the military?" Maggie asked.

He nodded. "I'm here to sell Gran's house."

"You're leaving soon, then," she said.

"Probably."

Did he see relief in her eyes? Why would she care if he stayed or left? She had once, but that was a long time ago. He hadn't intended to look her up while he was in town. As he'd passed by earlier, hidden in the milling crowd, he'd spotted her bright-red curls. Speaking to her had been the furthest thing from his mind, but something about her had drawn him like a beacon. She was a beckoning spot of color in his black, white and gray world.

Was it her hair, the shade of stubbornness? Her huge eyes—not quite green or brown, but with flecks of gold tossed into the mix. Maybe it was that tempting little body any red-blooded man would yearn to hold. She was compact and curvy. And her snug white T-shirt with the rodeo logo didn't hide much. He hadn't missed the way she'd crossed her arms over her chest earlier. It was the first time in a long time he was grateful he had an eye for detail.

What had compelled him to walk over to say hello? Maybe the way she caught her full bottom lip between her teeth—he remembered she did that when she was nervous—and she was doing it now. But none of the above explained why a man trained to endure and deflect interrogation had felt compelled to answer a little girl's questions. Not one training session had included techniques on resisting a child with big blue eyes and her mother's curls.

"Where did you go?" Faith asked him.

With an effort he pulled his thoughts from Maggie's sweet little shape and full sexy mouth to look at the girl. "Hmm?"

"You said you've been gone. Where?"

He stuck his fingertips into the pockets of his denims. "Everywhere."

Maggie turned a stern look on the girl. "Faith, the rodeo is almost over. I need you to help me pack up. Then it's home for you and bed."

"But, Mo-om, I'm not ready."

"I don't recall asking if you were ready. It's time to go."

"But school's out."

"I have to work tomorrow. And you've got to go to camp."

Jack wanted to tell the kid to just do it. In the army, a soldier never argued with a direct order. But this wasn't the military. Civilian life made him feel like a hick at a tea party.

Faith kicked the dirt and defiantly looked at her

mother. "But I didn't get to thank Jack yet. He saved my life."

That reminded him. Right after he'd plucked her out of the stock pen, the kid had said something odd. "What are 'dire consequences'?" he asked her mother.

"What?" Maggie looked at him as if he had two heads. "I think you know what the words mean."

"Yeah. But what specifically. When I picked her up, she saw you and said it was time to suffer dire consequences."

Maggie laughed, a merry, musical, sound that bumped up against his ice-cold soul. He swore he could almost hear the sound of breaking glass, and the sensation of fresh, cool air against his hot skin. He must be losing his mind—along with the rest of himself.

Amused, Maggie shook her head. "The last thing I said to her was that if she didn't stay within sight of the booth, she was going to suffer dire consequences," she explained.

"So what is that?" he asked. Just curious, he told himself. It wasn't like he felt any sympathy for the kid. He'd just met her. And she'd argued with a direct order from her commanding officer. He supposed that was normal for a kid. But he wouldn't know about that; he didn't do the kid thing.

But he did do consequences and he'd seen too many since he'd left Destiny. Enough to last him two lifetimes. Pain, suffering and death. He could never forget. He couldn't help wondering what this beautiful, innocent little girl considered dire—as far as consequences in her safe world were concerned.

"I haven't decided yet." Maggie met his gaze as she caught the corner of her bottom lip between her teeth—again. She was pretty nervous about something, he thought. "But thanks for reminding me."

"I couldn't have reminded you if Faith hadn't mentioned it," he pointed out. He was trying to help the kid while at the same time struggling to ignore the way Maggie's nervous habit made him want to taste her mouth.

Would she cut the kid some slack for voluntarily bringing it up? What kind of disciplinarian was she? He'd heard that when people who broke the rules as kids had kids of their own, they tended to act like a dictator trying to prevent a military takeover. He remembered teenage Maggie sneaking out to meet him. She'd been a good kid and he'd been her walk on the wild side. Her chance at defiance. But it had meant a lot to him. It was personal. He couldn't remember the last time someone had made a loner like him personal.

They'd gone to the same high school, and both rodeoed. Her parents had forbidden her to see him because of his bad-boy reputation. They'd been right, but that hadn't stopped stubborn, hardheaded Maggie Benson. And he still couldn't help being glad about that. Did Maggie's daughter take after her? Or her father?

That pulled him up short as a lassoed calf. Who *was* Faith's father?

The question stirred something inside him, the ashes of feelings that had burned out a long time ago.

Maggie put her hands on her hips. "Faith Elizabeth, go stay with Jensen Stevens until I come and get you. If you don't—"

"I know," the girl mumbled, digging the toe of her grungy white sneaker into the red dirt. "Dire consequences."

"That's right," Maggie confirmed. "Don't make me tell you what they are."

With head hanging and her hands in her pockets, the kid started to walk away. Stopping suddenly, she turned and smiled, a punch-to-the-gut beautiful smile that was one hundred percent her mother. "Thanks, Jack—"

"Mr. Riley," her mother corrected.

"Captain Riley," he clarified. "But Jack is okay."

Faith slid her mother a slightly rebellious look. "It was nice to meet you, Jack. Thanks for saving me. I hope I see you again. 'Bye."

"'Bye," he answered.

He watched Maggie watch her daughter. "How old is she?" he asked.

Her shoulders visibly tensed. She took a deep breath, then slowly released it. "Nine."

He did the math and his heart stuttered for a moment. Then he shook his head. Maggie would have told him. He remembered her saying she'd gotten over him. Must have been right away. Because up until then, she'd filled every letter with how much she loved and missed him. She must have met someone who'd made her forget about him right after she'd gotten her letter back, the one he'd marked Return to Sender. He'd wanted her to forget about him and move on. He had no right to feel anything because she'd done just that.

So why did he have to remember that just before he'd left, they'd been as physically close as a man and woman could be? She'd insisted on giving herself to him even though he'd tried to make her see that she was too young. In his gut he'd known being with her that way was wrong. But stubborn Maggie had dug in her heels and wouldn't take no for an answer. It would have taken more willpower than he possessed to turn away from the temptation she was back then. Still was, he corrected.

He found it oddly comforting that some things didn't change. She was a unique combination of spirit, sex appeal and sass.

And she'd written that she loved him and always would. Now he'd discovered that her declarations had been short-lived. But, even if he wished it could have been different, he wasn't entitled to regrets. He'd made his bed ten years ago and he had to suffer the consequences. A woman like Maggie and a child like Faith would never be possible for an empty-hearted man like him.

But he couldn't help wondering where the girl's father was. Maggie had asked him what he'd been up to for the past ten years. He'd wanted to know if there was anyone special in her life. But he hadn't inquired.

His training hadn't included polite social skills. It had been more along the lines of three hundred ways to kill a man with his bare hands. Or how to fit in without drawing attention to himself.

"Nine years old," he repeated. He catalogued the expression on Maggie's face and figured she probably didn't even realize she looked defensive. The expression was identical to Faith's when she'd decided her back was against the wall and she'd best do what her mother said. "She reminds me of you."

"Really?" She looked surprised, and relieved. "How?"

"Spirited. Willful. Beautiful."

He hadn't meant to say that. He couldn't remember the last time he'd said anything without calculating first.

Pink deepened in her cheeks, but she met his gaze dead-on. "You think I'm beautiful?"

"Yeah." He shrugged. "But I didn't think you were married."

"I don't recall you asking," she countered.

He nodded toward her left hand. "No wedding band."

"Ah," she said. "You thought right. I'm not married."

"Divorced?"

She hesitated. "No."

He raised an eyebrow. "It's got to be one or the other, Maggie."

"No, it doesn't. Not if I've never been married." She didn't look away and her small, pointed chin lifted slightly in the same rebellious gesture that he'd just seen on her daughter.

So she'd had Faith outside of marriage vows. That must have fried her folks, as protective as they were. What about the rest of the people in town? Had they been rough on her? She'd said her business had been around for five years, so if they had been, it was ancient history.

But damn it, that thinking was all a smoke screen. Typical of the coldhearted man he'd become, he couldn't stop the feeling of satisfaction that she'd never married. But that meant she'd done it alone—not the conceiving part, the raising part. And it ticked him off that a guy would use Maggie, then walk out on her.

"Do I know her father?" It was none of his business, but he couldn't stop the question.

Her face went white. "No one knows her father."

"Not exactly. *You* do."

"I'll clarify. I've never told anyone who her father is." Her hands were shaking.

"Not ever? Not even your folks?" He found that hard to believe.

"Not a soul." Color flushed back into her cheeks, but again he admired the fact that she didn't look away.

He wanted to ask why she'd kept such sensitive information to herself. He wanted to demand that she tell him the guy's name so he could make the creep sorry for deserting her. But he didn't ask questions. If anyone understood the necessity of keeping a secret, it was him.

"Guess you've got your reasons" was all he could say.

The whole time they'd been talking, spectators had been wandering by. Jack had been aware of announcements over the public address system. From time to time, static crackled in the night air. Now he heard a female voice say, "I love you, Mitch."

"That sounded like Taylor," Maggie said.

Jack glanced at the bleachers and noticed that all the spectators were turned to watch Mitch Rafferty and Taylor Stevens in the corral. He recognized them from the newspaper photo he'd told Maggie about. A buzz started in the crowd. After several moments it got louder and more widespread. Finally he figured out what they were repeating over and over— "Kiss her."

At that moment a big burly cowboy lugging a saddle walked behind Maggie and pushed her forward. Automatically Jack's arms went around her to keep her from falling. The man's mumbled apology penetrated part of Jack's consciousness. But it was the very small part *not* taken up with wondering if an all-grown-up Maggie tasted different. The crowd was chanting even louder now and far be it from him to singlehandedly curb mob rule.

He stared into Maggie's wide eyes. She swallowed once, and ran her tongue along her top lip. The movement was like kerosene to the sparks of his awareness. He went hot all over. Discipline had been his middle name for the last ten years. But a short time with Maggie had sent his self-restraint into the dumper. For the life of him, he couldn't seem to care.

Before he could talk himself out of it, he lowered his mouth to hers. The sweetness of it mustered a moan deep in his chest. He slid his arm around her waist and settled her more securely against him. He traced her bottom lip and her mouth opened, allowing him access.

He dipped inside the moist, honeyed interior. With her breasts pressed against him, he felt the rapid rise and fall of her chest. Satisfaction sluiced through him. This was a replay from all those years ago and felt even better now than it had then. He could still turn her warm and willing in his arms with just a touch. He lifted his head and opened his eyes in time to see that Faith had disobeyed orders.

"I guess that's how *you* thank him for saving me," she said.

"Faith," Maggie gasped, then pushed against his chest, urging him to release her.

He let her go and side by side they both met the gaze of her daughter.

"I—I thought I told you to stay at my booth," Maggie managed to get out.

Jack heard the slightly breathless quality to her voice

and, God help him, couldn't stop the intense feeling of pleasure that coursed through him at the sound.

"Mo-om, you said to stay with Jensen."

"She's at the booth," Maggie said.

"No, she's not," the child answered.

"Who's manning the booth?"

"Ronnie Slyder's mom."

"Where's Jensen?" Maggie demanded.

Faith rolled her eyes. "In the stands."

Maggie rested her hands on her hips. "Why aren't you with her as ordered?"

"I was. But now she's talking prudence with Sheriff O'Connor," she said.

"Jurisprudence?" Maggie asked.

"Yeah. That's what Jensen called it." She frowned. "But the sheriff is mad about something."

"What?" Maggie asked.

The girl shrugged. "I don't know. He said something about being served. But he didn't have any food."

"Was it about papers?"

"Yeah, I think he mentioned some papers."

"How did you figure that out?" Jack questioned.

Maggie met his gaze. "Sometimes you have to read between the lines. Jensen is an attorney now. I understand she's taking some time off from her Dallas job and is staying with her sister Taylor on the ranch."

"Good information. I'm going to need some legal help with Gran's estate," he said. "Although I don't think it's complicated and wouldn't take much of her time."

"She'd probably be happy to give you a hand."

"I want to go home, Mom."

"Okay."

"Then I guess this is goodbye." Again, he thought.

And probably for the best after that kiss. She'd given him a cheap lesson. She always could make him forget himself before he could say damn the torpedoes, full speed ahead. Which was why he'd returned her letter ten years ago. He'd had an opportunity to be good at something and needed to cut any personal ties that weren't family. He hadn't trusted himself to resist any request she would make to get back together.

A feeling of loneliness surrounded him, a sensation he hadn't ever felt before. The last time he'd said goodbye to Maggie, he'd had high hopes for making something of his life. Now he couldn't shake the feeling he should have grabbed hold of her and hung on for all he was worth.

"Where are you staying, Jack?" Maggie put her hand on her daughter's shoulder and her knuckles went white.

"Gran's house."

"Then it's not goodbye."

"What do you mean?"

"Faith and I live next door. It's more like, 'Howdy, neighbor.'"

Chapter 3

Maggie rubbed her gritty, sleep-deprived eyes then stared for the umpteenth time at her stalled computer monitor. If she could have frozen her mind as solid as that screen, she'd have slept like a baby last night instead of tossing and turning and thinking about Jack Riley. Worrying the tie of her lightweight cotton robe, she decided having this technical problem to focus on was a blessing in disguise. The silver lining to her Jack Riley cloud. Technical glitches almost took her mind off the fact that Wild Jack was back. She was nearly frustrated enough to overlook all the possible ramifications of that fact.

"Control, Alt, Delete works for everything," she said to the screen and put action to the words. When there was no change, she sighed and shook her head. "Why should this be different from the rest of my life? I'm so together even my computer is frozen."

Then, being Maggie, she went from the general to the specific. Specifically that kiss. Why had he done it?

She'd heard nothing from the man for ten years, then he shows up and kisses her. What's she supposed to do with that? For one thing, she had to tell him the truth about Faith.

There was a soft tap on the front door and she figured her hearing must be as tired as her eyes. It was the crack of dawn—way too early for anyone to show up at her door. Even her daughter the early bird was still asleep.

Maggie padded barefoot to the front door. Standing on tiptoe, she peeked through the peephole and recognized Jack. Instantly she moved out of sight, as if he could see her, and pressed her back to the door, trying to control her hammering heart. What was he doing here? For several moments she toyed with the idea of not answering. He didn't know her routine. For all he knew, she and Faith could be gone. Then she remembered the evidence of her presence was parked in the driveway. Real soon she was going to have to clean out her garage so she could get her car in there.

But she could still be asleep for all he knew. Then she sighed. Cowardice wasn't her stock in trade. Sooner or later she had to face him. Wouldn't it be best to get it over with?

She removed the chain lock and dead bolt and opened the door. Smiling she said, "Good morning, Jack."

"Maggie."

"You're up early."

He nodded. "I don't need much sleep."

"Wish I could say that." She looked up at him—way up—and pulled her cotton robe more snugly across her bosom. For a man who got by on little sleep, he looked awfully good. His hair was short and she couldn't tell if he'd combed it or not. She tried to picture him in uniform, but the thought wouldn't focus. She'd only ever seen him dressed as he was now—smooth worn jeans and a white T-shirt. The sleeves snugly surrounded his bulging biceps, the soft clingy material molded to the muscles and contours of his impressive chest.

"How did you know I was awake?" she asked.

"Heard your slider open a little while ago."

The man must have ears like one of those very perceptive wild animals whose survival depended on their keen sense of hearing. She'd have to remember that. "What can I do for you?"

Tell him, the good angel perched on her right shoulder insisted. *He has a right to know.*

The devil on her left shoulder chimed in, *It isn't your fault he never received your letter. He dropped out of sight.*

True, she thought, very much liking that left-shoulder devil. The problem was, he was in her sight now, and he had a right to know.

"Can I borrow some coffee? If you've got extra?"

It would be so easy to give him enough grounds for a pot and send him on his way. But for the life of her, Maggie couldn't do it. Before she thought it to death, or turned into one of those scary characters who answered the voices in her head, she made up her mind.

"I can do better than that. Would you like a cup of already brewed coffee?"

"Yeah. Thanks."

"Come on in." After he did, she closed the door and locked it again. "Follow me. The kitchen is this way."

Feeling self-conscious in her flimsy nightclothes, she

led the way through her living room to her kitchen at the back of the house. Shorty pajamas barely concealed by a thin cotton robe wasn't exactly proper attire for receiving gentleman guests. Then again, Jack had seen her in a lot less ten years ago. Did that really count now?

She reached into the cupboard, annoyed because she hadn't arranged the cups on a lower shelf. She had the worst feeling that she was getting "cheeky" with the man from her past. In spite of it, she refused to give in to the sensation by pulling at the hem of her robe. But her cheeks—the ones on her face—burned.

With her back to him still, she busied herself with pouring steaming black coffee into a large mug. If she was lucky, by the time she was finished she'd have a cooling off period and could turn to look at him with her dignity shored up.

"Here you go," she said, handing him the cup. "Do you need milk or sugar?"

He shook his head, then blew on the coffee. "Thanks."

"You're welcome."

He looked around her kitchen. "This is nice. Homey."

She followed his gaze. Oak cabinets above and below a beige ceramic-tiled counter filled two walls. At the end closest to the family room there was a matching built-in desk holding her computer. Beyond that, was the open slider to her backyard, letting in air that was the coolest it would be all day. A tiny butcher-block island stood in the center of the room.

"I like it," she said. "The best part is, I made it happen all by myself."

Could she have sounded more defensive? she

wondered. She looked at Jack to see if he'd noticed. He was watching her, but she couldn't read his expression. Only once last night had she been able to detect a stirring of emotion in him, when she'd introduced her daughter. Maggie didn't have any problem deciphering her own reaction to him.

Sooty shadows of stubble sprinkled his cheeks and jaw, clueing her that he hadn't shaved yet. How intimate was this? Sharing coffee with a man in her kitchen before his morning shave, as if… Don't go there, Maggie, she ordered herself.

She dated occasionally, but she'd be lying if she said she'd ever seen a more masculine man in her kitchen. Last night at the rodeo, her attraction had kicked in instantly and she'd chalked it up to a dreamlike quality connected to the night. But it was morning now and the sun was up. With his dusting of whiskers and hair tousled from sleep, Jack Riley was still the best-looking dream she'd ever had. The handsomest man she'd ever seen.

And she was the woman who had a secret he had a right to know.

Maggie stood with her back to the counter and Jack leaned a shoulder against the wall that separated kitchen and family room. As they sipped their coffee, an awkward silence developed between them. In the old days they'd had ways to fill the silence—ways having everything to do with mouths and tongues and frantic hands that couldn't touch each other enough. Did he remember?

Jack met her gaze for a moment and stuck the fingertips of his free hand into his jeans' pocket. "Maggie, I—"

"Hmm?"

"I want to explain what happened."

"What? When?"

"Ten years ago. Why I didn't come back."

"You don't have to—"

"Yeah, I do."

She nodded, then blew on her coffee. "Okay. What about it?"

"You probably don't remember the letter I wrote."

Her breath caught at the instantly recalled pain of the words he'd written. *Go on with your life.... Not fair to you.... Can't ask you to wait.*

"Refresh my memory," she said, then sucked air into her lungs.

"I had certain—skills and qualifications my commanding officer recognized and tapped. I was recommended for Special Forces. A mission."

"How nice for you."

He sipped his coffee, covering any reaction to her sarcasm. "They hand-picked the candidates and each was chosen on the basis of qualifications and no personal ties."

Just the one you turned your back on because you didn't know. And the one you overlooked because you did, she silently amended.

"Go on," she urged.

"They encouraged us to sever any ties we could because the mission was dangerous. We didn't know if we'd make it back."

"But you did."

"Yeah."

He stared into his coffee at things only he could see.

A muscle in his cheek contracted and somehow she knew his memories were painful ones.

"And you didn't get in touch," she added.

He met her gaze then but she couldn't see past the shadows. "I knew it wouldn't be the last mission. Personal relationships weren't encouraged."

"I see."

"My career took off."

"Congratulations."

"I found something I was good at, Mags."

"And what is that?" she asked.

One corner of his mouth quirked up. "I could tell you but then I'd have to kill you."

She knew he was joking, but only partly. In his circumspect way, he was telling her he was one of those men who went where others feared to go. One who kept the gray area safe for Mom, apple pie and the girl he left behind. But there was someone else he'd left behind and he needed to know about her.

Only how could she tell him? He couldn't even tell her specifics about what he did for a living. He was hiding things. Dangerous things? He was her daughter's father. And Maggie couldn't deny she was still attracted to him. But the truth was too sensitive to just drop on him out of the blue. Or at all? What did she really know about him? She knew he wasn't staying. He might not even want to know.

"It wasn't fair to ask you to wait," he finished.

"Thanks for making the decision for me."

Maggie had intended the words to be light and breezy, but they'd sounded sarcastic and just this side of hateful. She was ten years too late in fussing at him for not getting in touch. But the depth and power of the emotions churning inside her confirmed that she still had unresolved feelings.

"Can I warm your coffee?" she asked.

When he nodded, she grabbed the pot and walked over to him. She had to touch him, wrap her hand around his to hold his cup steady. Meeting his gaze, she saw the dark intensity in his eyes and wondered again what the sensitive mission and all the others since had entailed. Her first obligation was to protect Faith. Before she brought father and daughter together, she needed to know more about him. Besides, he said he'd only be there temporarily. Was it right to reveal this secret knowing Faith would be heartbroken when he left her? If anyone knew how that felt, it was Maggie.

She took one step away from him, then another and another until she was across the room and could form words again.

"Can you tell me what skills brought you to your commanding officer's attention? Or would you have to kill me then, too?"

"I don't think that's classified. It was actually two things. Physical—"

"There's a surprise." As soon as the words were out of her mouth she wanted them back with a fervor she reserved only for chocolate. "What I meant was, you were in pretty good shape. From rodeoing. As I recall," she finished lamely.

A slow, sexy grin curved up the corners of his lips. "Endurance was a factor. And intensity."

She'd been the focus of that intensity once upon a time. It had been pretty seductive. And the primary reason why she'd been relieved when he'd said he wouldn't be in Destiny for long. She didn't want to chance having such concentrated scrutiny land on her for any extended length of time. Historically, she didn't handle it well.

"What other 'know-how' brought you attention?"

"I took to computers like a wild mustang takes to the open range."

"There's that Texas boy I knew and—"

What? Loved? Not anymore. No way, no how. Nope.

She shook her head. "So you're good with those ornery little contraptions? Maybe you're just the man I need."

One dark eyebrow rose. "Oh?"

She ignored the way her heart hammered, her hands shook and her knees wobbled. "Y-yeah. My computer is a mean-tempered, lazy, stubborn, good-for-nothing pile of chips, hard drive and disks."

"Froze up on you?"

"That seems like a big leap."

"Nine times out of ten the level of frustration you just expressed usually means the computer froze up. Want me to take a look?"

"More than you could possibly know."

He walked to the desk and leaned over to study the screen. He turned the machine off and waited several moments before booting it back up again. Not that she even wanted to get close, but before she could move in to peek over his shoulder, he touched some keys, then straightened and looked at her.

"I think it will work for you now. If you talk nice."

"What did you do?" she asked reverently. Then she held up a hand. "Never mind. If you tell me you'd probably have to kill me and I really don't want to know that badly."

He laughed. "It's easy."

"Maybe for you. I don't mind admitting I'm technologically challenged. And I have a great deal of respect for people like you."

His smile dimmed, then died. What had she said?

"Thanks for the coffee, Maggie." He walked to the sink and rinsed out his cup. "I'll get out of your hair. You have to go to work and Faith has camp."

"How did you know that?"

"You mentioned it last night, when you said it was time to go home."

"Oh." He was a sharp one. She would tuck the information away. "We've got time. I could fix you breakfast—"

He shook his head. "I have an appointment. But thanks anyway. I'll let myself out."

And then he was gone. The man dropped in and out of her life with about as much notice and the same potentially destructive force as a stealth bomber.

"Faith, it's time to go."

Maggie put the finishing touches on her daughter's lunch and snapped the lid closed on her lunch box. As she put the dirty peanut butter knife in the sink, she noticed the mug Jack had used just a short time before. She rubbed her finger around the rim. It was cold; his mouth was warm. She remembered from last night. She'd never forgotten.

"Faith Elizabeth, we're going to be late."

The sound of the slider made her turn around. "What were you doing outside?" Maggie asked.

"Jensen is next door talking to Jack."

Her daughter stood in front of her, the clean denim shorts and powder blue T-shirt she'd put on a short while ago now sporting dirt stains.

"How do you know this?" Maggie asked.

"I heard them talking," she answered vaguely, digging the toe of her sneaker into the vinyl kitchen flooring.

"Have you been climbing the tree between the yards and spying on him?"

The child shook her head and Maggie marveled at how well she did the wide-eyed-innocent act. Did the ability come from herself—or Jack?

"I didn't have to climb the tree, Mom. He was talking really loud. Something about the damned will. What does that mean?"

"First of all, that's not a word we repeat, young lady."

"Will?"

"You know good and well that's not the one. Second, he was talking about his grandmother's will, what she wanted to happen with her things after she died."

Faith's blue eyes suddenly filled with shadows, so like the way her father's had just a short while ago. "I miss her, Mom."

"Me, too, sweetie."

"Do you think Jack is sad, too?"

"I'm sure he is. He was very close to her when he was younger."

"I wonder why he didn't come back," Faith said.

Because finding something he was good at was more important than his grandmother. Or me, Maggie thought sadly.

"I couldn't say."

"While I was in the backyard," the child continued, careful not to incriminate herself, "I heard them say something about selling the house."

"It makes sense. Jack's job is in the army. He doesn't need to keep it," Maggie explained.

"Sure he does."

"Why? Because a person can't have too many houses?"

"Yeah," Faith agreed. "I hope he doesn't sell it."

"Even to someone who might have a little girl just your age?"

"I've already got friends my age. Kasey and Stacey are my best friends—ever."

"I can't imagine Jack hanging on to the house. Like you said—he hasn't come back until now. Why wouldn't he sell it?"

Faith shrugged her thin shoulders. "I dunno. But I hope he keeps it. I wish he'd stay, Mom."

Uh-oh, Maggie thought. Incoming—as in heartbreak. Faith couldn't possibly have any clue about her relationship to the mysterious stranger next door. Yet she'd begun a bond. No doubt because he'd plucked her out of the stock pen last night. In her daughter's eyes, he was the proverbial man in the white hat. And she didn't know what to say to insulate the child's fragile feelings.

"C'mon, sweetpea. We have to get going. And there's no time for you to change out of those clothes you got tree dirt on. If I've told you once, I've said it a hundred times—stay out of the tree. You're going to get hurt."

"Aw, Mom, climbing trees is as easy as pie."

"Here's your lunch box." When the child took it, Maggie touched her shoulder. "No argument. No editorializing. Just do as I say—no climbing trees."

"Yes'm."

They hurried out the front door and Maggie turned to lock it. Then she moved down the steps and to the car. As she opened her door, she noticed Jensen walking to her BMW parked at the curb in front of the house next door.

"Hey, Jen," she called. "How's it going?"

The other woman turned, then smiled and waved when recognition hit. "Hi, Maggie." She put on her sunglasses. "I'm fine. Did you hear? Taylor and Mitch got engaged last night."

"Give them my best wishes."

"I will, but right now Jack could use a friend."

"What's wrong?"

Jensen tucked a strand of mahogany hair behind her ear. "You'll have to ask him. If he wants to say anything, he will. Attorney-client privilege." She shrugged. "You off to work?"

"Yeah. What about you?"

"I'm going into Destiny to scout possible locations for a branch office for my firm."

"Really? I didn't know you were expanding."

She looked down at her hips, then grinned. "Not me personally. This area is growing fast and the partners see a lot of potential."

"Would you be working out of the new office?" Maggie asked.

"I don't know. It's all still in the planning stages." Her clipped tone and tight mouth told Maggie that her friend had some reservations.

If she did decide to stay in town and work the new office, Maggie would be surprised. Jensen associated Destiny with some unpleasant memories. The husband she'd lost after just a single year together had grown up here, too. Maggie wondered if she knew that she was lucky to have had even a year with the love of her life. It was more than she'd had—not that Jack was the love of her life. But there was something to be said for closure.

"Hey, I don't want to keep you two. Hi, Faith," Jensen called.

"Hi," the girl said. They watched Jensen get into her car and drive away. "Mom, there's Jack."

Maggie shifted and saw him on the front porch. He looked—what? Angry? Annoyed? Like a volcano about to erupt? Sad? She and Faith had had some time to deal with the older woman's death, but she suspected that he was just beginning to. Did he need someone to talk to?

Faith ran around the car and raced up the steps next door. "Hi, Jack."

"Hey," he said. "Don't you have to go to camp?"

She nodded. "I wanted to see if you were okay about G.G. Dot."

"You called her that before. Why?"

Maggie rested her hand on her daughter's shoulder. "Your grandmother didn't like being called Dottie or Mrs. Riley and especially not 'ma'am.'" That produced a slight smile from him. "She said she was old enough to be Faith's great-grandmother and asked us to shorten that to G.G. Dot."

Maggie prayed she'd put the right amount of off-handed casual into the explanation. What she'd told him was the truth—just not quite all of it.

"Are you all right, Jack? Faith said she heard loud voices—"

"Yeah," the child chimed in. "You said something about the damned will—"

"That's enough," Maggie said. "Remember what I told you about that word?"

"Yes'm," she said, hanging her head.

"Go sit in the car and wait for me."

"Yes'm." She started down the steps. "'Bye, Jack."

"'Bye." He looked at Maggie. "She heard me?"

"I'm sorry. She likes to climb the tree in our backyard. There's one big limb that overhangs your side. I've told her over and over not to go up there. I'm terrified she's going to get hurt. But—"

"She's stubborn. Like her mother."

Maggie glanced over her shoulder at the child who'd just slammed the car door. "I guess the fruit doesn't fall far from the tree."

"Good one," he said, the corner of his mouth quirking up.

"Thanks. But seriously, are you okay?"

"No." He shook his head. "I just found out something that really ticked me off."

She held her breath. Did he know about Faith? Had G.G. Dot put something in her will? Maggie could feel the pulse at the base of her neck pounding. "Do y-you want to tell me what's wrong?"

"You bet I do," he said angrily.

Chapter 4

Jack briefly wondered why Maggie was staring at him as if he'd cut the pigtails off Faith's favorite doll. He couldn't blame her. His show of temper was completely out of character. Army training and ten years of structured military life had ingrained the habit to not tip off his feelings. And he was good at what he did. But the terms of the will had shaken him more than a little—specifically the directive from his grandmother—G.G. Dot.

That sounded so like her—to treat Faith as if she was a member of the family. Dottie Riley had never made a secret of the fact that she'd wanted him to settle down and have a family of his own. Since he hadn't, Gran obviously had adopted Maggie and Faith when they'd moved in next door.

"Jack, what's wrong?" Maggie asked. "Say something. You're scaring me."

That just goes to show what happened when he was released into polite society. You can take the boy out of the military, but you can't take the military out of the boy. How could he handle living up to the rules his grandmother had set? How could he not?

"Jack?" Maggie put her hand on his arm. "Tell me."

She looked as if she were bracing for a life-altering announcement. Actually, only his life would be affected, and not permanently.

"Okay, Mags. Here goes. By the terms of the will, I have to live in Gran's house for a year before I can sell it."

He watched Maggie's face, waiting for her reaction. The fear in her expression faded to puzzlement. Frankly he'd expected the fear to stay put—because he would be next door. He looked closer and noticed the splash of freckles across her small nose, the sunglasses perched like a headband to keep her red curls tamed, the flecks of light and dark green and gold that made up the hazel in her eyes. She was full of hues and shades of color—a firecracker.

And he was stuck there for a year. It was wrong. He didn't belong here. It had been less than twenty-four hours and already Faith was in hot water for repeating a word she'd heard him say. And Maggie would tempt a card-carrying, dyed-in-the-wool, vows-of-poverty, chastity-and-obedience-dedicated monk to question his calling. His grandmother must have been one cookie short of a dozen when she'd had this will drawn up.

"I don't understand." Maggie blinked and shook her head. "It doesn't make any sense. How can she force you to stay? What does it say?"

"The terms state that if I fail to live in the house for three hundred sixty five consecutive days, the house will be sold and the money donated to Destiny's rock museum."

"Are you sure?" She took the sunglasses from the top of her head and put them over her eyes.

He leaned one shoulder against the porch overhang support and continued to stare at her. Between her hair and eyes she was all the colors of the rainbow. Until seeing her again, he hadn't realized how colorless his world had become. But circumstances had made him what he was. Black, white and gray were safer for him and for everyone else. What had his grandmother been thinking with this will thing?

"Yeah, I'm sure."

"The town has a rock museum?"

"There must be one," he said. "I guess. How should I know? The point is that Jensen said the will is simple and straightforward. It doesn't take a lawyer to interpret. If I don't live here for a year, some stupid useless rocks will be the beneficiary of her estate." He studied her mouth, the way it curved up at the corners. "Are you laughing at me, Maggie?"

"No. Of course not. Heaven forbid." But her lips tilted up as far as they could go *without* laughing. "So what are you going to do?"

"I don't have a choice. I can't abide the thought of the proceeds from the house going to anything so frivolous. And I suspect she knew I would feel that way. I'm going to live in the house."

"But what about the army?" she protested. "Don't you have an obligation?"

"I've given ten years to the army and never asked for

special favors." His mind was racing. "Gran had something up her sleeve, some reason she wanted to keep me here. I just wish I knew what it was."

"I know."

"You do?" He straightened and stared at her. "Did she say something to you? Care to enlighten me?"

Maggie retreated a step. Jack swore she looked like she hadn't meant for that to slip out. Like she wanted those words back in the worst way.

"She didn't confide in me. That's not what I meant." Maggie glanced over her shoulder. "It's just a guess really. I think she wanted you to spend some time here in Destiny."

"Why?"

"I guess to remind you about family—"

"There's nothing for me here now. She was the last of my family."

"It's more than that. I think she wanted you to remember that Destiny is your roots." Maggie shrugged.

Her lifting of shoulders was meant to be casual, but she looked tense enough to snap in two. Especially when he'd made the remark about Gran being the last of his family. "Destiny has nothing for me. Not anymore."

"You can argue till hell freezes over," Maggie pointed out, "but G.G. Dot is sitting on a cloud in heaven and she's having the last laugh."

"Now there's an interesting visual," he commented.

"Unless you're willing to turn this house over to Rocks 'R' Us, you've got some decisions to make. So what are you going to do? About the army, I mean. Don't they have rules about not coming back when you're supposed to?"

"It's time I called in some favors. I'll have to extend my leave."

"Yeah, a three-hundred-and-sixty-five-day extension. Will that be a problem?" she asked, trying to act casual.

What was going on with Maggie? She wasn't laughing now. It had finally sunk in that he wasn't leaving right away. But why should she care if he hung around for a year? She didn't know how he'd changed. If he could help it, she never would. He could hide in the jungle indefinitely, Gran's house in Destiny was hardly even a challenge.

He folded his arms over his chest. "I'll arrange for a leave of absence. For personal reasons. Since I've been threatening to quit I don't think they'll mind giving me some time off. But I don't want to hold you up. Don't you have to get to work?"

"Yeah. But now I have to ask why?"

"Why what?"

"The part about threatening to quit the army?"

"For me," he said. "Before it's too late."

"Too late? I don't understand."

"You don't want to know. I've done some things that would probably shock you, Maggie."

"Like what, Jack?" She rested her sunglasses on top of her head and met his gaze without flinching.

He ran a hand through his hair. That was the last thing he'd intended to say. A soldier didn't question orders; a soldier just carried them out. His military service was none of her business. Or maybe it was more that he didn't want to confess and see shock and disapproval chase away her trusting innocence.

"Believe me. It's best if you don't know."

She continued to meet his gaze with a direct one of her own. "I have a feeling you're being too hard on yourself."

"Why?"

"Because you always were."

"It was hard not to be. I had a reputation. For God's sake, your parents ordered you not to see me."

One corner of her mouth tipped up. "Yeah. Unlike you, I guess I wouldn't have made a very good soldier."

It came back in a flash—waiting around the corner from her house while she sneaked out to meet him. The anticipation. The exhilaration when he'd pulled her into his arms. They hadn't been able to get enough of each other.

"Trust me, ten years of soldiering changes a person."

"Ten years changes anyone. I'm not the same person I was when you left. And I don't have any idea what you're like now. But if you abide by the terms of the will, you'll be here for a while. I'd like to get to know you—the way you are now. It's about time."

"Why do you say that?" he asked, curious at her phrasing.

"I-it just seems that—Dottie would have wanted it that way," she finished.

Considering the will, he couldn't argue with that logic. But she deserved to know what kind of man was living next door to her and her daughter.

"For starters, my language leaves something to be desired in polite society."

"Last time I checked, colorful language wasn't a hanging offense. And I don't think there's anything you could say that I haven't already heard."

"What about Faith? I'm sorry she got in trouble for repeating something I said."

Maggie smiled, a look filled with affection he'd only seen her use on Faith. "One thing about my daughter—she doesn't need help getting into trouble. Whatever your sins, Jack, make sure they're yours alone. Don't take on more than you should. Faith is gifted at pushing the envelope. She knew good and well to not say that word. Besides, you can't be held responsible for her eavesdropping. She was testing me."

"How?"

"Trying to shock me—to see what I would do."

"And?"

"I didn't let her down. She got a reaction, swift and sure." Maggie grinned. "I've done a lot of reading. Children beg for boundaries. They break rules hoping that a parent will lower the boom as a way of demonstrating how much they're loved."

"Really?" He rubbed the back of his neck. "Sounds pretty complicated."

"Not really. The point is—I think you need to cut yourself some slack, Jack."

"If you knew me, really knew me, you wouldn't say that."

He studied Maggie, who opened her mouth as if to say more then abruptly shut it. "Look, I don't want to hold you up. You've obviously got things to do. Faith is waiting."

As if to underscore his point, her car horn blared, making her jump. She glanced at her daughter and waved. "Hold your horses. I'm coming." Then she turned back to him. "You're right. I have to go. See you later."

"'Bye."

He watched her walk down the steps, leather sandals on her feet and her trim little figure showcased perfectly in a denim sundress. Red polish made her toes look as sassy and colorful as the rest of her. He couldn't help but wonder what his life would have been like if he hadn't left town. Would their illicit liaison have been discovered? Would he and Maggie be together now?

That line of thought was pointless. It didn't matter. Ten years had turned him into a man she wouldn't want. No amount of wishing would change that fact.

For the next three hundred and sixty-four days, he needed to batten down the hatches, guard his perimeter and bolster the fortifications. When he'd walked away from Destiny all those years ago, he'd left behind any chance for a normal life. When he walked away a year from now after surveillance of a normal life, he wouldn't leave Maggie's heart—or his own—in rubble.

"Hi, Maggie."

Startled at Jack's voice, Maggie's hand flailed out and knocked over her coffee cup. Fortunately for her antiquated computer it went in the opposite direction of the keyboard.

"Good grief, Jack," she said, jumping up to grab the roll of paper towels on the shelf beneath the cash register. She went back to her small desk in the corner and blotted the brown liquid seeping into her paperwork. "The least you could do is let a person know you're there. Maybe you should wear a bell around your neck."

He came around the counter and ripped a paper towel off the roll. Lifting the keyboard out of the way, he helped her mop up the liquid.

"Maybe you need a bell over the door so you know when you're not alone."

"This is Destiny. Folks don't need a bell. They announce their presence—with their mouth."

"I'll remember that."

Maggie's impression when she'd left him about two hours ago was that he would hunker down in the house. Part of the reason he'd startled her so was that he was the last person she'd expected to see.

She put a hand on her hip. "What are you doing here? Couldn't stay away, huh?"

"Yeah."

She'd been kidding, but he didn't look like he was. "Yeah? I thought you Special Forces types could be still like a statue for years and only come up for air when the coast was clear."

Humor flickered in his expression before he tamped it down. "A trained operative reconnoiters first."

"Would you mind translating for those of us who aren't trained?"

"We snoop out our surroundings to see where an enemy attack might come from."

She glanced around her shop with its displays of beaded bags and embroidered jackets. T-shirts were arranged on a wonderful antique dressing table and a chest of drawers held odds and ends—This 'N That.

"Well, you certainly picked the right place to sniff out an enemy stronghold. God knows there's a secret agent lurking behind every sequined shirt and antique mirror in the place. It's cluttered, a good environment for your archenemy covert operative to find the perfect hiding place."

"Are you making fun of me?" He folded his arms over his chest.

"You bet I am."

"No one makes fun of me."

"Don't look now, but I think I just did." She glanced up at him and couldn't resist lifting her chin just a fraction. "Someone needs to. You take yourself far too seriously."

"I see. And you arrived at this diagnosis after how many years of schooling?"

She could lie, but that wasn't her style. At least not about the things she could safely tell him. "I dropped out of high school. Later I took an equivalency and received credit so I could take some business classes."

"So you have no training in psychiatry?"

"Not formal, no." He looked momentarily puzzled, but fortunately didn't ask why a college prep student like her had dropped out. "Although I'm pretty intuitive."

"Well, there's credentials."

"Are you making fun of me?" she asked, letting a wet paper towel fall into her trash.

"You bet I am."

"Okay. Good. You learn fast."

"That's what my commanding officer said after basic. The rest, as they say, is history." He glanced at her desk. "So what are you doing?"

"It's a slow day. The championships ended last night and most of the town's visitors left. I need to catch up on my computer work."

"I could help."

Maggie happened to be studying his expression and that was the only reason she saw the surprise on his face. He hadn't meant to say that. She'd bet her best-selling jacket design on that. So why had he? Should she let him off the hook? That would be the easy way out. For her and him. It had never been her style before. Why should she start now?

She needed to get to know him. She had a decision to make and that would be impossible without data. The only way to get the info she needed about Jack was to spend time with him. Besides, if he could do as much for her computer here at the shop as he had for the one at home, she would be in his debt forever.

"I'd appreciate any help you could give me," she answered honestly.

He walked over to the keyboard and pressed a couple keys. "I could upgrade your system if you'd like."

"What's wrong with the system I've got?"

"For one thing it's so old I doubt you're compatible with any equipment or software in the free world."

"You're exaggerating."

"I never exaggerate."

"There's a surprise," she said dryly. "Am I going to have to spend money on it?"

"Do you want to?"

She shook her head. "Not if I can help it. It's not in my budget."

"Then, no." He sat in her chair and started fiddling with the machine.

"Are you going to program it so I can't use it? Will it go berserk and destroy the town of Destiny?"

He shot her a wry glance. "You've been watching too many cheesy TV movies of the week."

"No way. I'm serious. When you're finished, will I need a doctorate in computer technology to know how many beaded bags are in my inventory?"

"I will tutor you regarding any changes that I make."

"Fair enough."

Gosh, he was cute. In one of those moments in time that stand still, she realized he was cute as could be and she loved teasing the serious out of him. She'd been attracted to him in high school. He'd been the only time she'd ever disobeyed her parents. Now, a decade later she was still attracted to him. She couldn't decide whether or not that should be comforting.

As Jack's fingers flew over the keys, Maggie realized that as much as she wished to stare at His Cuteness, it wasn't the smartest thing she could do. She busied herself storing inventory and putting away merchandise that she'd brought back from her booth at last night's rodeo. She thought he might chat, but the silence from his side of the room was deafening. Either he couldn't talk and compute at the same time, or he didn't want to talk to her at all.

This might be a good time to change her window display. After all, it would be Fourth of July pretty soon. She pulled out a white T-shirt, the front of which was emblazoned with a silver-red-and-blue sequined flag. She undressed the mannequin in the window, then redressed it in the sparkling shirt and a coordinating pair of white shorts. For the final touch, she added a red-beaded shoulder bag. Behind the mannequin, she tacked up some other decorative shirts—one with a lighted firecracker, another with Uncle Sam's face, and, of course, the Statue of Liberty—all the symbols of the freedom to be celebrated several weeks from now.

It occurred to her that Jack had worked to safeguard the liberty that she and everyone else in Destiny took for granted. He'd hinted that his soul was a lost cause. She thought he was wrong, but even if he wasn't, she figured she owed him. For a lot of things.

When she turned to climb out of the window, she found him standing there watching her. He held out his hand to assist her down.

"Thanks. Is my computer done already?"

"It's uploading some stuff. And it's slow," he added.

"So am I. Why should it be faster than I am?"

He didn't answer. Instead he studied her in that serious way she was beginning to recognize.

"Go ahead," she suggested.

"What?"

"You want to ask me a question. Go ahead."

"Why isn't there a man in your life?"

That wasn't the question she'd been expecting. Compared to that, solving a calculus equation would be a walk in the park. Finally she settled on evasion.

"What makes you think there isn't?"

"I just know."

"You've been here less than twenty-four hours. We shared a cup of coffee together this morning, then I chatted with you on your front porch. *How* could you possibly know anything about me?"

"No guy stuff in your family room. Just girly things. Instinct tells me there's no man in your life. And it doesn't make sense," he added.

"Why not?"

He only hesitated a moment before answering. "Because you're beautiful, smart and funny. You should be beating the guys off with a stick."

She was too stunned to reply. The man who buried

his feelings so deep the average person would mistake him for a robot had just paid her a compliment. How did she respond to that?

"I'm picky," was all she could think of to say.

"All evidence to the contrary."

"What does that mean?"

"Faith. I did the math. She was conceived right after I left. In your letters you promised to love me forever."

"I was a kid, Jack. Besides, you dumped me. Remember?"

Had he guessed her secret? Her heart pounded and she was hot all over. How would he take the news? He'd sounded almost sad that she hadn't fulfilled her promise about loving him. She didn't know what to think. Did he believe he'd made a mistake? Would he ask for a "do over"?

"I remember what I did." He sighed and stared out the window at downtown Destiny. "And it was for the best. I learned not to count on a future beyond tomorrow."

"Jack, I—"

He held up a hand. "Forget it, Mags. If that sounded like a criticism— Believe me, it wasn't. And I'm not fishing for information. You would have told me if she was mine. It would be a miracle if a guy like me was responsible for someone as wonderful as Faith. Miracles are something else I learned not to count on."

Tell him, Maggie.

He'd just handed her the perfect opportunity. But she couldn't. Not yet. She needed to know more about him. Why did he think he didn't deserve Faith? She hadn't known him well a decade ago, what kind of man was he now? She had an obligation to find out more. Once she took the step, there was no going back.

"Why are you so cynical, Jack?"

"Why aren't you, Maggie?"

"Because I believe the best about people until they give me reason not to."

"You're asking to get kicked in the teeth."

"I think I'm meeting people halfway."

He shook his head. "You need a keeper, Mags."

"You applying for the job?"

"As much as I need something to fill my time while I wait for the year to be up, I think you're a bigger job than I can handle."

"No guts, no glory," she said.

"If the combat boot fits, a smart man keeps his mouth shut."

"What does that mean?"

"Beats the heck out of me." He looked at her for several moments. "Are you hungry?"

She would swear that he was looking at her mouth when he'd said the words. Suddenly her heart began to beat like the bass drum leading the Independence Day parade. "I am," she whispered, her mouth so dry the inside of her throat felt like sandpaper.

"Would you have lunch with me?"

"I would."

Maggie knew she had no business being this happy that Jack Riley had invited her to spend time with him. She felt like a giddy schoolgirl again. God help her.

Chapter 5

Jack sat across from Maggie at the Road Kill Café, downtown Destiny's only eatery. They shared a booth in a semi-secluded corner, the table between them covered with a red-and-white checkered cloth. The restaurant's interior reminded him of the generic Old West saloon portrayed in every B Western he'd ever seen. Wooden floor, long bar with brass footrail and round tables surrounded by barrel-backed chairs dotting the center of the room.

"So this is the famous, or should I say infamous, Road Kill Café," he commented, looking everywhere but at her.

"Wasn't this here ten years ago?" she asked.

"I'm not sure."

There was a lot of that going around. He wasn't sure why he'd volunteered for lunch duty with Maggie. When he finally looked at her and she smiled, he knew. The answer was as clear and bright as her face. This was a chance to bask in her warmth—for just a little while. He couldn't make himself go back to his bleak world and it was all Maggie's fault. She'd brought vibrant shades of color back into his life.

If he felt that strongly about her after less than twenty-four hours, what would happen in a year? But three hundred and sixty-five days was all it could be. He'd been raised an army brat without the kind of roots too deep to be pulled. When his dad retired, they'd lived a few years in Destiny. At his father's insistence, Jack had enlisted after high school. Permanent wasn't in his vocabulary. It was stupid to start something he couldn't finish.

After today, he would just have to avoid her. He'd been the beneficiary of the best covert training in the world. Eluding one small green-eyed redhead should be a walk in the park. So why did it feel like he was running for his life?

"Earth to Jack."

"Hmm? Did you say something?"

He focused on her and tried to find a safe zone. Her silky hair made him want to run his fingers through the fiery strands. Those big eyes of hers, flecked with gold and different shades of green, threatened to pull him in and drown him. But her mouth was by far the most dangerous territory. Her lush, full lips made him think about twisted sheets and long, slow kisses on a warm summer night.

She smiled. "I said, in spite of the name, the food here is good."

"As compared to what?"

"Probably what you're used to eating. K-rations?" She

tipped her head and her halo of curls tilted to the side, brushing her shoulder. "Isn't that what military food is called?"

"Actually, it's MREs—meals ready to eat. I think military food is an oxymoron."

"I thought that was military intelligence."

He held up a finger. "Now you're getting nasty, and personal."

"Aha. So you're in military intelligence." She made a cross with two fingers. "Do you have to kill me now?"

Not unless he could do it with kisses, he thought.

Halt. On the double. He wasn't going there. And after this, he would keep to himself if it took every last ounce of willpower he had. The next time he got the wild idea to go into town and invite Maggie to lunch, he would make an appointment to have his head examined instead. He was probably long overdue for a visit to the shrink.

But he couldn't help smiling at her. And damn, it felt good. "Relax, Maggie. I didn't confirm your guess about what I do. So there will be no termination."

"Well, that's a relief."

Jack realized he'd all but forgotten how carefree felt. He couldn't remember the last time he'd teased, joked and shared a laugh with a woman. He was rusty and a little slow, but he still recognized fun. Maggie pulled him out of himself just by being Maggie. Surely this brief contact wouldn't taint her? Surely the gray area where he'd lived for the last ten years couldn't harm her. Not from such a short time in her company?

A waitress in jeans walked up to the table. Her red

T-shirt sported an armadillo wearing a Stetson. "Howdy, Maggie. Are you going to introduce me to the fella?"

"Hey, Bonnie. He's an old friend from high school. Jack Riley, meet Bonnie Potts, owner, waitress and hostess of the Road Kill Café."

"Hi," he said, giving her a casual salute.

"Nice to meet you, Jack. What can I get y'all to drink?"

He looked at Maggie. "What'll it be?"

"I'd like sweet tea."

"A sweet tea for the lady and I think I'll have the same," he said. "It's been a long time since I've been anywhere there was the possibility of getting anything resembling a good glass of iced tea."

"Coming right up," Bonnie said with a grin. The pretty auburn-haired, blue-eyed woman pulled a couple of plastic-coated menus from beneath her arm and handed them over. "Have a look at these and I'll be back in a little bit to take your orders."

Jack opened his menu. It was safer to look there than at the woman sitting across from him. Why was she dangerous? How could she threaten him? How could one small female pose any threat? Samson had probably asked the same thing about Delilah. It was a question that still didn't have an answer.

Jack just knew spending time with Maggie would be the most dangerous op he'd been involved in for a long time. He was a man of action. He formulated a plan, then carried it out. The best he could come up with at the moment was to finish lunch, check her computer, then get the heck out of town before she was the wiser. Wiser about what? If he knew the answer to that question, there would probably be a way to sidestep the minefield that was Maggie.

"So what do you recommend?" he asked, not looking up from his menu.

"Something tells me you wouldn't eat quiche."

He lowered the plastic menu just enough to meet her gaze and give her a wry look. "What does that mean?" The twinkle in her hazel eyes made him want to smile.

"Good heavens, I should think that would be obvious."

"I'm going to take a wild guess here. As in, real men don't eat quiche?"

"And I thought I was being subtle. I'll have to watch my step."

"And stereotyping."

"So you're getting the quiche?" she asked.

"No way. I see a burger combo and it's got my name on it," he answered.

She laughed and the sound was so full of carefree joy, somehow it made him ache deep inside. He couldn't remember the last time anyone had touched him there. The place was so deep sunlight never reached it, yet Maggie had breached his defenses and marched right in without firing a shot.

She studied her menu then closed it. "You know, I haven't had my quota of raw meat today. That sounds really good. I think I'll have a burger, too."

"Okay."

It suddenly occurred to Jack that this was the first time he and Maggie had been out in public. They'd kept their brief but memorable relationship secret. At the time, that had made it even more exciting, as if the girl

Maggie had been needed anything to make her more exciting to him. But the fact remained, she'd been afraid her folks would find out about them. He'd had a couple brushes with the sheriff, giving him a reputation, and she had insisted on furtive meetings. Who knew he'd be so good at clandestine that he would make a career out of it?

And lose himself in the process.

A bell tinkled as the café door opened. Sheriff Grady O'Connor walked in, looking official in his khaki uniform. He checked out the room, then nodded to Jack and headed in his direction.

He stopped at the end of the booth. "If it isn't Wild Jack Riley."

"Grady." He held out his hand and the lawman shook it. "It's been a long time."

"Yeah." He looked from him to Maggie and back again. "I didn't know you knew our Maggie."

Our Maggie? Was the sheriff implying that he would stand between her and harm? Was he warning Jack off? He'd rather cut off his right arm than hurt Maggie.

Jack met her gaze and swore he saw apprehension lurking in the green-gold depths of her eyes. Apparently she had the law on her side. He had the feeling if he fought the law, the law would win. So what was she afraid of?

He looked at Grady. "Maggie and I were friends. Ten years ago."

The sheriff nodded. "I saw you two talking at the rodeo last night."

"Renewing the acquaintance," Jack explained.

"Mind if I join you?" he asked.

"By all means," Maggie said, sliding over to make room for him.

Something hot and hard tightened in Jack's chest. He was used to *not* feeling anything and it took him a couple beats to recognize jealousy. It didn't make sense. Grady was a friend from high school and their bond went deep. Besides, there was nothing romantic between himself and Maggie. But the power of his reaction forced Jack to admit that he *really* disliked watching the sheriff's tan sleeve brush the bare skin of her arm. He checked out the ring finger of Grady's left hand, and silently cursed when he found no band of gold. Not even a tan line indicating there had been one there recently.

"So what are you up to these days, Jack? Still in the army? Special operations?"

He nodded. "That about covers it."

"That covers nothing," Maggie said. "For a job description, it's clear as mud. But I'll tell you one thing. The man is a computer guru."

"I wouldn't say that—"

She gave him a sassy look. "Of course not. You don't say much of anything." She glanced at the sheriff. "But, Grady, if I hadn't seen it with my own eyes, I wouldn't believe it. He unfroze my home computer with just a flick of his wrist."

When she touched the other man's arm in an innocent, friendly gesture, a white-hot poker pierced Jack's chest.

"And as we speak, he's updating my system at the shop. The man is a bona fide computer geek."

"Is that so?" Grady said, meeting his gaze.

Jack rested his arm along the top of the seat back.

"I'm not comfortable with the geek part, but I know my way around a hard drive."

"I may need your help with something. Can I talk to you later?"

"Sure."

Bonnie Potts returned with notepad in hand and the three of them ordered the burger combo. About forty minutes later Maggie finished the last of her tea and excused herself to get back to the shop.

Grady slid from the booth to let her out. "Do you mind if I talk to your computer guy for a couple minutes?"

"You're the sheriff." She met Jack's gaze. "But don't abandon me, big guy."

Abandon. Interesting choice of words, he thought. "I'll see you in a few minutes."

When Maggie left she took his carefree mood with her. Jack tried to ignore the feeling.

"Jack, I've got a favor to ask," Grady said.

"Shoot." He toyed with the end of his fork, resting on his empty plate.

"You've been gone for ten years, so I'm not sure how much of my story you know. But I've got twin girls."

"Yeah. I saw them at the rodeo. Hanging out with Maggie's daughter Faith."

"Yeah. The girls are practically inseparable." He took a deep breath then said, "Billy Bob Adams is suing me for custody of them."

Jack froze. Hazy memories surfaced. "Does this have anything to do with what his brother did to Lacey that night at the lake. It's ten years ago now, right?"

Grady nodded. "He's Zach Adams's brother. It's the only connection. But I don't have a clue why he's doing this. Zach's been gone for nine years. But so's Lacey.

What could he hope to gain after all this time? Surely he doesn't really want the kids. He'll never get his hands on them," Grady vowed. "Not while I have breath left in my body."

Jack was awed by the depth of feeling in his friend, by his instinct to protect his kids. "How can I help?"

"I've done a background check on him with the computer at the cop shop."

"Anything turn up?"

The sheriff shook his head. "If you're as good as Maggie says, and I have a feeling she doesn't even know the half of it, you may be just what I need. Can you do a private search?"

"Yeah. I can go places you don't even know exist. I'll see what I can find."

"Can we keep this between the two of us?"

Jack nodded. If there was anything he was good at, it was covert. It had started with Maggie. Then the army tapped his talents and turned him into a loner. He'd been seduced by how good he was.

So good, he was sentenced to life outside the fire.

When Maggie arrived home after nine-thirty, the front porch light was on. She had needed to stay late at the shop to get some work done and had called Zoe Slyder, one of the teenage girls she relied on for baby-sitting to stay with Faith. It was times like this when she missed Dottie Riley the most. Jack's grandmother had picked up the slack for her and it had been a comfort to know her daughter was with family. Even if Dottie hadn't known.

It was past Faith's bedtime, so Maggie quietly let

herself in and tiptoed through the living room to the family room and kitchen. "Zoe," she called softly.

The TV was on low and Maggie stopped short when she saw, stretched out on her couch, a sound-asleep Jack Riley. Apparently there were times when he needed more than a little sleep. She wondered what he was doing there, but didn't have the heart to wake him to ask.

Silently she went down the hall to Faith's room and peeked inside. She let out a long relieved breath when she saw her peacefully sleeping daughter. Explanations about changes in plans could wait now that she knew her child was okay. She pulled the pink sheet up and tucked it around Faith's sturdy little body. It wasn't even close to being cold, but it was a mom thing she could never resist doing. Somehow that flimsy little sheet was symbolic protection from any threat—real or imagined.

If only she could as easily protect her from real life, Maggie thought.

She moved quietly back into the family room and stood just a foot away from where Jack was sleeping. She hadn't been able to get him out of her mind all day. His black hair, blue eyes and rare playful smiles made her yearn for things she hadn't in ten years. The memory of Jack's mysterious remark that a guy like him couldn't be responsible for someone as wonderful as Faith squeezed the tenderness from her heart. He needed to know the truth. She had no right to keep it a secret and she'd made up her mind to tell him the very next time she saw him.

She just hadn't expected to see him again so soon.

Soundlessly she moved forward and reached out a hand to gently touch him awake. Before her fingers made contact, he grabbed her wrist. The next thing she knew, he'd hauled her onto the couch and was pressing her into the cushions using the weight of his body to hold her motionless. That and his forearm, which was flat against her windpipe. The vivid, intense look in his eyes—like a predator challenging his prey—scared her.

"Jack," she croaked.

"Shoot, Maggie." He moved his arm, allowing her to breathe and talk.

"You were expecting Destiny's resident stalker/slasher?"

"You can't be too careful." The words were teasing; the look on his face was anything but. Then he let out a long breath and with it the tension seemed to drain out of him. One corner of his mouth quirked up. "How was your day?"

Apparently they weren't going to address the fact that he'd just greeted her like he was taking down the enemy. Two could play this game. "My day was just fine, thanks. And yours?"

"Can't complain." He released her wrist and slid his hand to her waist, moving his thumb up and down over her rib cage in a subtle caress beneath her breast. There was a slight shift in his expression—from peril to passion. "In fact, my day just now improved one hundred percent."

He rolled to his side, easing some of his weight off her, but not loosening his grip. Tucking his arm beneath her, he snuggled her more securely to his chest. She could feel him pressing against her leg.

Jack Riley wanted *her.* Good Lord. She should be outraged, but she needed to catch her breath first. And slow her heart down to normal. And somehow control the trembling that was spreading through her like wildfire. Then she would be outraged.

He slid his hand up and covered her breast with his palm. "Your heart is pounding," he said, his voice husky and deep.

"There's a good reason for that."

"Me?" A slow half smile curved the corners of his mouth.

"Yes, you. But don't let it go to your head. You scared the bejeezus out of me."

"I know." He sighed and his grin faded. "I'm sorry, Maggie."

"So," she whispered, "are you going to let me up?"

He shook his head. "Not yet."

He looked as if he wanted to swallow her whole and for the life of her she couldn't find the will to mind. It seemed like forever and back before he finally lowered his head and touched his lips to hers. The contact was electric. Her eyelids drifted closed, and brilliant light flashed across the darkness. Her already-inflamed breathing cranked upward like a kerosene-soaked wick. When his clever fingers kneaded her breast through the denim of her sundress, liquid fire poured through her. She arched her back and settled herself more surely into his palm.

It was like going home again, to a long-remembered haven and finding it changed—for the better. She managed to free one of her hands from between them and rest it against the muscled wall of his chest.

She smiled against his lips. "Your heart is pounding too. Did I scare the bejeezus out of big, strong you?"

"Darn right."

"I'll try not to—"

"Over my dead body," he said, and kissed her again.

Maggie felt every ounce of concentration and focus in the touch of his mouth to hers. That was different. He'd kissed her ten years ago until she went up in flames. It was even better now. He was no longer a wiry teenager. He was a man and she couldn't help being fascinated by how big he was. How incredibly wide and hard and strong. His shoulders hunched forward, seeming to surround her, to shelter her in his arms. The predator as protector? Why had she never felt so safe as she did at this moment?

When his tongue stroked her lower lip, she surrendered without a fight and opened to admit him. He took possession of her mouth, caressing the interior with single-minded determination. Yet she felt him hold back. That was something he hadn't done when they were teenagers. He'd lacked the experience and art to wait and woo and whittle away a woman's will. Not anymore. She could feel his arms trembling from his effort to hold back. As he tucked her hair behind her ear, his hand shook slightly, showing her the strain he put on himself to wait to make it better.

Maggie slid her hand around his neck and brushed her fingers over the razor-short hair at his nape. She arched closer to him, her breasts pressing against the hard wall of his chest. She nearly lost control when he gently touched his tongue to an almost-forgotten spot just beneath her ear. Obviously Jack hadn't forgotten. She wanted—

"Mo-om?" Faith's voice came from down the hall.

Jack pushed away and he was on his feet in a heartbeat. Before she even had a chance to feel the absence of his warmth, he held a hand down to her and helped her to stand.

"Mom? Jack?" Faith stood in the doorway and sleepily rubbed her eyes. "What are you guys doing?"

Maggie looked at Jack and saw the spark in his eyes. "N-nothing, sweetie. Did you have a bad dream?"

She wouldn't be the only one. What in the world was she thinking? Kissing Jack Riley. The answer was clear. She hadn't been thinking—at least not with her head. Dormant hormones were dangerous hormones. Her last coherent thought had been that she owed him the truth. The next minute she'd flipped, literally, and wound up with him on top of her. One minute he'd been peacefully sleeping, the next he'd turned into a warrior who could snap her like a dry twig. How in the world could she share with this relative stranger the secret that would no doubt insinuate him more intimately into Faith's life?

Before she did, there was a lot more Maggie needed to know about Jack Riley.

"Did you have a nightmare?" she asked her daughter again.

Faith shook her head. "I just wanted to say good-night to you."

"Okay. I'll tuck you back in bed." Unable to meet Jack's gaze, she walked to her daughter and guided her to her room.

Faith hopped back into her bed. "Is it okay that Jack was here, Mom?"

No, it wasn't okay, she wanted to say. What was she thinking? Maggie wanted to ask.

"Why *was* he here?" Maggie couldn't believe she hadn't demanded this explanation from him. What kind of mother was she? The kind who was still easily distracted by the way her child's father kissed.

"Zoe Slyder was babysitting, but she had to leave. Her brother—remember he was the one who got hurt by the bull at the rodeo?"

Maggie nodded. "I remember. What about him?"

"He got out of the hospital. Her mom wanted her to be there when he got home. She wouldn't have left, but Jack said he wouldn't mind staying here until you got home."

"And whose idea was it for him to come over?"

Faith met her gaze. "Mine. I figured it would be okay as long as I wasn't alone. I remembered when G.G. Dot was alive and used to stay with me when you worked late. Then I remembered Jack. He's a perfectly good babysitter and he's right next door. Are you mad because I didn't call, Mom?"

Maggie had had the same thoughts about Dottie. How could she fault Faith for thinking the same thing? Although father and daughter didn't know it, the child was still with family. She sighed. "It's all right, Faith."

When had she learned to lie so well? Nothing was all right. In fact it couldn't have been more all wrong.

"I like Jack," Faith commented.

"I'm glad." She tucked the sheet around her daughter. "What did you guys do?"

Faith shrugged. "We watched some Disney videos. He fixed me hot dogs for dinner. And we played catch with the softball in the backyard before it got too dark."

"Sounds like fun."

"Yeah. He's pretty cool."

Cool wasn't exactly the way Maggie would describe him. He made her feel hot as a sinner on a preacher's knee. She hadn't felt like this since high school when she'd been head over heels in forbidden love. Until a few moments ago she'd thought nothing could be as out of control as what they'd done way back when. She was mistaken—and then some. But it ended here. She would put on the brakes. As soon as her daughter was settled back in bed, she would tell Jack in no uncertain terms that he wasn't to kiss her ever again.

"Go back to sleep, Faithy," she said. She leaned down and kissed her daughter's cheek. "Good night."

"'Night, Mommy."

"Don't let the bed bugs bite." She stood and watched the little girl roll to her side, facing the wall.

Maggie stood for a few moments watching. Then she sighed, realizing that she was just putting off the inevitable. Sooner or later she had to go back out there and face Jack and the fact that she'd come this close to making a fool of herself over him. Again. And she had to tell him it couldn't happen again.

It wasn't bad enough that she didn't know anything about him. But what made her kick herself from here to next Tuesday was the fact that he wasn't staying in Destiny. Worse, he made no secret of the fact that he didn't want to stay. He was bent out of shape because Dottie had backed him into a corner to keep him there. For a year. Then he would go back to what he was good at. Where would that leave her?

High, dry and heartbroken.

She'd done that once. She wouldn't do it again. No matter how good a kisser he was.

She walked back into the family room, prepared to talk to Jack. But he was gone. Part of her was relieved.

The other part of her cried out in protest at being alone. He'd turned his back on her again.

"Oh, Jack," she whispered. "I wish you could care enough to stay."

Chapter 6

In the backyard under the shade of a spreading oak, Jack braced his feet hip-width apart for another go-round. He raised his arms even with his shoulders and slashed through the air with his right hand. Just call me grace, he thought dismally. The self-defense move was worse than a beginner, which he definitely wasn't. He'd been working out all morning but his form and concentration had gone to hell in a handbasket. What was wrong with him today?

Was it the Texas heat and humidity? The fact that he'd kissed Maggie the night before? Her daughter spying on him from the knothole in the fence between their properties? Or all of the above?

Behind him he heard leaves rustle in the tree limb that hung over the fence. Faith was getting brave. She'd been watching for a while now without saying a word but he almost felt her curiosity as a palpable thing. He sensed that she was finally going to say something.

"Whatcha doin'?" she asked. "Looks like some kind of fightin'."

"It is."

He turned toward her and grabbed the towel he'd hung over the wrought-iron patio chair. After wiping the sweat from his face, he draped the terry cloth around his neck and walked over to talk to her.

"Is your mom working?" he asked, looking up at her perched on the tree limb.

"Yeah. How'd you know?"

"Because she doesn't want you climbing the tree." He lifted his arms toward her. "I'll help you down."

"Are you doin' karate?" she asked without moving.

He sighed and rested his hands on his hips. "Sort of. Is Zoe Slyder babysitting you?"

"Nope." She shook the dark curls out of her face. Then she scooted forward a bit and swung one small leg over the limb to straddle it on his side of the fence.

"Is anyone at your house?"

"Other than me?"

She was something else. He raised one eyebrow that, in the military, never failed to intimidate whoever needed intimidating. "Yeah," he said. "Other than you."

"Nope."

She wasn't impressed. Apparently the eyebrow needed work. "Does your mother know you're home alone?"

"Nope."

"Where are you supposed to be?"

"At day camp."

"Why aren't you there?"

"Logan Peterson was makin' fun of me. I decided to walk home."

He had a feeling she'd left out a whole big part in the middle of that story. But that wasn't his problem. What he had to worry about was getting her out of this tree without any casualties.

She shifted her weight and wobbled precariously. His heart lurched as she grabbed at the branch over her head. "Do you have any kids, Jack?"

"No." A flanking maneuver and nicely done, he thought. "You need to call your mom? You can use my phone."

"Do you want kids?"

Another parry. Again, nicely done. "I haven't thought about it." Much, he added silently. Never give the opposing force any quarter. No latitude for maneuverability.

"Kids are a good thing," she said.

"I don't doubt it." He wiped the sweat beading on his forehead. "Now, about calling your mom. My phone is inside. Would you like to use it?"

"Nope."

"Can you get into your house?"

"Yup. Mom leaves a key hidden in the backyard. I was getting it when I saw you doin' kung fu. Would you show me how?"

"It's probably not something your mom would want you to know."

"Sure she would."

About as much as she liked the language the kid had overheard him use, he guessed. Maggie had her hands full with this one. Anger welled up in him again for the guy who'd deserted and left her with a child to raise all by herself. Since the two were on their own, Maggie had to work to support them, leaving this independent little girl in the care of others. Who apparently weren't watching her, he thought grimly. He wondered if anyone from the camp had realized yet that she was AWOL.

"Do you know anything about your father, Faith?" Two could play this game, he thought, getting more curious.

Her brow furrowed for a moment, then she shook her head. "Not much."

"What did your mom tell you?"

"That he didn't abandon me."

"How does she know that?"

She shrugged. The movement tilted her slightly off balance and she slid to the side. "That was close," she said, righting herself.

He'd reached his arms out to catch her, but he would have been too late. As his heart rate kicked up, he wondered just how long he should let this go on before he reached up and hauled her out of that tree.

"You shouldn't be up there. Your mom doesn't want you in the tree."

"How do you know?" She held onto the branch with her hands and went backward, then let her arms dangle while her legs kept her from falling.

"I heard her tell you to get down."

Faith's black curls reached for the ground as she hung suspended like a monkey. "She worries too much. I'm fine."

Could a mother worry too much? Especially about a kid who was obviously in training to be a circus acrobat?

He wouldn't know. He'd never known his mother. She'd died when he was born. "So how do you know your dad didn't abandon you?"

"Because he didn't know about me."

Very little shocked Jack, but that did. "How could he not know about you?"

"Mom didn't tell him. She said he left town before she could."

"She didn't get in touch with him?" he asked.

Jack was getting a feeling that made the hair at his nape prickle. He'd been in dangerous situations many times and had learned to rely on all five senses and another that was nothing more than gut instinct. It made his skin crawl, but more than once had saved his life. His skin was crawling now. Big time.

Faith grabbed onto the branch and pulled herself into a sitting position, making him wish she was working with a net. "Are you hungry?" she asked. "I am."

He was hungry, all right. For information. She'd tapped into his curiosity in a big way.

"I asked you a question, Faith. Your mother didn't get in touch with your father?"

"I guess not."

"She didn't try?"

"I don't want to talk about it anymore. I'm hungry."

She started to back away, sliding across the limb backward. When she was on her side of the fence, she executed an awkward turn. The next thing Jack knew there was a rustle of leaves, a frightened cry from the child and a loud thump. Then silence.

"Faith? Are you okay?"

No answer. Quickly he scaled the fence and

dropped down beside the child who lay on the ground. "Faith!"

If only his grandmother were still here. He'd missed her over the years, but never more than he did right now. His first-aid training kicked in and he ran his hands over her arms and legs to check for broken bones. There didn't seem to be any, but she wasn't moving. What worried him the most was that the little chatterbox wasn't talking. Her eyes were open. That was a good sign. She looked scared.

"Faith? Can you hear me?"

"Can't breathe," she whispered.

"You got the wind knocked out of you. That's all. You're okay. Relax."

Sucking in air, she grabbed for his hand. "You're not— Don't go—"

"I won't. I know this is a hard one for you, but don't talk."

She nodded. Her face was white. The freckles marching across her little nose stood out starkly against the pale skin. He had to contact Maggie. But he couldn't leave Faith alone. He checked her more closely, and saw a gash in her knee and a goose egg forming on her forehead.

"Can you move your arms and legs?" he asked.

She showed him that she could and he nodded with satisfaction and let out a long breath. Now what? He could call the paramedics and the child's mother. But by the time help arrived, he could have scooped her up, driven her to Destiny and had her in the urgent care clinic, which was right next door to her mother.

He lifted her into his arms. "Okay, Faith. Here's what we're going to do..."

* * *

On the third ring Maggie picked up the shop phone. "This 'N That," she said.

"Maggie, this is Christy at Destiny Day Camp."

"Hi, Christy. Is something wrong?"

"We can't find Faith."

Maggie's heart dropped. "Are you sure she's not just hiding in the bathroom?"

"She and Logan Peterson had a disagreement. We put both children in time-out. When we gathered everyone together for lunch, she was gone. Mrs. Shirley and I think she probably walked home again. We called the sheriff's office. Sheriff O'Connor said he would ride around and look for her. Don't worry."

"Thanks, Christy. I'll close up the shop and go look for her, too."

"Is there a neighbor you can call to check the house?"

Jack. Maggie's heart plummeted for the second time in less than a minute. An instant visual of tangled arms and legs flashed through her mind. The last thing she wanted was to call him.

"Yes. I'll phone my next-door neighbor to have a look."

"Let us know if you find her. We'll check the grounds here again in case we missed her. I'll let you know when she turns up."

"Okay."

Maggie clicked the Off button and started to dial G.G. Dot's number. She figured Jack probably hadn't changed it. Then through the window she saw him coming from the direction of the urgent care clinic next door to her shop. He was wearing black sweat shorts and a camouflage T-shirt that molded to every last muscle on his chest. She was around the counter in a flash as he opened the door.

"Jack, Faith's camp just phoned. She's gone. Have you—"

He nodded grimly. "I was just coming to tell you. I brought her in to the doc."

Maggie felt the blood drain from her face. "Oh, God. What—"

He was beside her in two strides, his big warm hands on her upper arms. Holding her. She was sure if it hadn't been for that, she would have fallen in a heap.

"I don't think it's serious, Mags. But I decided the fastest way to get you and help for Faith was to bring her into town."

"What happened?"

"She fell out of the tree."

"Oh, God—"

Maggie started to shake from head to toe. Taking a deep breath, she closed her eyes and pulled herself together with an effort. If she lost it, she'd be no help to her daughter.

"Okay," she said. When she opened her eyes, she looked into Jack's concerned blue gaze. He was there. God help her, she was glad he was there. "I'm all right now."

She grabbed her purse from the drawer of her computer desk and fished for her keys. After putting the Closed sign in the shop window, she locked up. Hurrying next door, she went into the clinic and up to the reception desk.

Without waiting, she slid back the glass. "Addie? Where's Faith?"

Addie Ledbetter, the plump, orange-haired nurse/office manager met her gaze. "In the exam room. Come on back, Maggie. Doctor Morgan is with her now."

Hannah Morgan had come back to Destiny to visit her mother. She'd filled in for Doc Holloway at the rodeo and was also seeing patients in his office while he was away on a family emergency. Faith had never been examined by anyone besides Doc. He had a lot of nerve being gone when they really needed him.

She followed the nurse down the hall, frantic to see her daughter, to see for herself that her child was all right. Addie opened the exam room door and stood aside for Maggie. Faith was lying on the paper-covered table, looking pale and pathetic.

"Faithy, sweetie. Are you okay?"

"Hi, Mom. I'm fine. Jack said the doctor should check me as a 'caution.'"

"Precaution. And Jack is absolutely right." Maggie glanced over her shoulder. He'd followed her.

"Jack put me on the table and said I'd suffer dire consequences if I moved before you got here and the doc said it was okay."

Maggie made a mental note to grin about that just as soon as she knew her child was okay. On that same list, she made a note to ground Faith for the rest of her life for disobeying a direct order and scaring her mom to death. But that was for later. Now she needed to be supportive. And there was something else she had to do.

She glanced at Jack, who ran a hand through his hair. "Thank you," she said.

He met her gaze as he folded his arms over his chest. "You're welcome. For what?"

"The camp counselor called and told me she was missing. When you came into the shop I was just phoning you to see if you'd seen her lurking around the house. Thanks for bringing her here. It was quick thinking."

"No problem. I tried to get her out of the tree. I knew you didn't want her climbing. I wish she hadn't fallen. If I'd only been more—"

He looked so worried and guilty. Both characteristics of a parent—a father. A wave of guilt washed over her that had nothing to do with Faith's accident and everything to do with telling him the truth. Which she would do very soon. But now wasn't the time.

Maggie put her hand on his arm. "At least a hundred times a day I wish I was more."

Before he could answer, the door opened and in walked a young blond-haired woman wearing a white lab coat, a stethoscope draped around her neck. She held out her hand to Maggie.

"Hi. I'm Hannah Morgan."

"Hi. I recognize you, Doctor," she said, shaking the other woman's hand.

"Addie pulled Faith's chart for me." She flipped some pages and said, "Dr. Holloway saw her a few months ago for stitches in her chin."

"That's right," Maggie confirmed. "She's sort of a regular."

"Well, let me take a look at our little daredevil. Hi, Faith. I'm Hannah."

"Hi," the little girl said.

"What happened?"

"I fell out of the tree."

The doctor shone a light into the girl's eyes, and

examined the bump on her forehead. “Did she lose consciousness?” Hannah asked, looking at Maggie.

Guilt washed over her again as she realized she couldn't answer the question. She looked at Jack. “Did she?”

“No.” He shook his head. “I was over the fence in seconds and her eyes were open.”

Hannah nodded. “That's very good.”

She checked Faith from head to toe, looking into her ears then noting the obvious scrapes on her legs. Finally, she looked at Maggie. “I don't think there's any serious damage. But that's an awfully big knot she's got there. I'd like to do a CAT scan, just to be on the safe side. We can do it here in the clinic.”

Maggie nodded. “Whatever you think best, Doctor.”

“Will it hurt?” Faith wanted to know.

“Nope. I promise you falling out of that tree hurt more than this will.”

“Okay,” the child agreed.

“I'll have the tech take her back.”

“Can I go with her?” Maggie asked.

“Sure. After we get the results, I'll be back in to talk to you.”

“Thanks.”

A few minutes after she left there was a knock on the door. A young woman opened it. “I'm Leigh Denton. This must be Faith.”

“Yeah,” the child said.

“I'm going to take you for a ride in this chair,” she said, pushing in a wheelchair.

“I can walk,” Faith answered.

“Sorry. It's the rules.” Leigh shrugged.

Jack moved forward. “Let me give you a hand.”

He lifted her from the exam table and set her in the chair. “Lead the way. And don’t pop any wheelies.”

Faith giggled as the technician wheeled her out the door and down a long hall to the rear of the office. Maggie followed along with Jack. He put his hand at the small of her back to guide her and she was grateful for his support. He could have fetched her, then excused himself. After all, he didn’t know yet that he was Faith’s father. And she’d assured him the accident wasn’t his fault. Still, he’d stayed. Maggie couldn’t help wondering why.

Leigh opened a door and led them into a waiting area with another hall in front of them. “This is as far as you can go. Make yourselves comfortable. And try not to worry.”

“Mission impossible. But thank you for taking such good care of her,” Maggie said, sincerely meaning every word.

The next moment the tech had wheeled Faith into a room and closed the door. Maggie was alone with Jack. Unable to sit still, she started to pace.

“She’s got a pretty hard head,” he offered.

Maggie stopped in front of him and looked up. “And you know this—how?”

“She’s your daughter.”

And yours, she wanted to say. But she didn’t want him to find out like that. She didn’t want to blurt out the information. It was important to set it up, to minimize shock. To deal with him gently.

“Are you implying that I’m hardheaded?” she asked.

“The fruit doesn’t fall—”

"Far from the tree," she finished.

"Sorry. Bad example."

"It's okay. That expression is so appropriate in this situation."

He reached out and pulled her into his arms, holding her against him. It felt so good not to be alone. In the beginning, when Faith was a baby, her mom and dad had been there for her. But it wasn't the same as having the support of the only other person who could care about this child as she did. This was the first time Jack had shared a parental crisis with her. Would it be easier—or harder if he knew the truth?

It was so good to have him there. He was so big, so solid. So strong. She would go to hell for being selfish while Faith was undergoing tests, but she couldn't help remembering the kiss they'd shared on her couch the night before. If Faith hadn't interrupted them when she had, Maggie wasn't sure she could have resisted Jack. She hadn't been able to turn him away a decade ago and the yearning she still felt for him seemed to have intensified in direct proportion to the number of years since she'd last seen him.

What would happen when she told him he was Faith's father?

She shook her head. One crisis at a time. When Faith got the all-clear, she would worry about the kinder, gentler way she was going to break the news.

The door opened and Leigh wheeled Faith into the waiting room. "We're finished. You guys can wait in the exam room. Follow me. This place is like a maze. When I first started working here, I felt like I had to drop a trail of crumbs to find my way out."

Maggie laughed. "Yeah. This is the first time we've been back here."

"That's a good thing."

A few minutes after they'd settled in the exam room, Hannah walked in and Addie followed her inside. "Everything looks fine. The nurse is going to clean up the scrapes on Faith's knees while I talk to the two of you in my office."

Maggie's stomach clenched, but she didn't dare start this conversation in front of her daughter. If it was bad news, she would figure out a way to break it to the child.

Jack took her hand and gave it a reassuring squeeze as they followed Hannah into an office. The top of the desk was obscured with papers and charts. A plush leather chair waited behind it. Hannah motioned to the two wing chairs in front of the desk. "Have a seat."

"I'm too nervous. Tell me, doctor. What is it?"

"Everything really is fine. I didn't mean to alarm you. Sometimes the kids get upset with scary medical stuff." She put the films up on the viewing board behind the desk then flipped on the light. "I did a training rotation in emergency medicine. These are textbook normal. No indication of traumatic or brain injury. She's good to go."

"Thank goodness," Maggie said, pressing a hand to her chest in relief.

"Yeah, thanks, Doc."

"You're welcome." Hannah looked at Jack. "It's amazing," she said, shaking her head.

"What?"

"Faith looks just like you."

Maggie's heart dropped. Her head snapped to the side

to gauge Jack's reaction. She opened her mouth to say something, but no words could make it past the lump in her throat.

Unaware of what she was doing, Hannah continued. "She's inherited your blue eyes, your black hair—although she's got her mother's curls. I understand you're career military."

"That's right."

"That would explain why Faith never shed a tear. Your daughter is quite a brave little soldier, too."

"My daughter?"

Maggie felt as if a boulder the size of Texas had just dropped on her chest. She looked at the astonishment in Jack's expression and knew he was about to deny the doctor's statement. But then he looked at her and his face turned to granite.

"My daughter," he said.

Chapter 7

Jack maintained surveillance through his front window until he saw Faith get in the car with her friend and the girl's mother pulled away from the curb. Earlier that day in the doctor's office, Maggie had pleaded with him to wait before asking questions. She didn't want to have that conversation in front of Faith. He agreed it would probably be for the best to discuss the situation when she wasn't around.

Damn right, he had questions. As angry as he was, he didn't think he could censor himself for a kid's ears. Maggie had said she would arrange something so that Faith would be gone. They could discuss everything in private. He waited until the car turned the corner.

Good to go, he thought.

He crossed his driveway and the SUV parked there, then went to Maggie's house and raised his hand to knock. Before his knuckles connected with wood, the door opened.

"Hi, Jack."

"Maggie."

"Come in," she said, pulling the door wide when she stepped back.

As he passed her, he caught a whiff of some sweet, flowery fragrance. It seemed innocent somehow. But that was impossible. After all, this was Maggie Benson. She was the furthest thing from innocent and honest. She'd lied to him for ten years.

But as he studied her now, he damned the fact that the sight of her still brightened his day. Whenever he looked at her he couldn't help but think sunshine. She was wearing yellow shorts made out of some clingy T-shirt material and a matching tank top that skimmed her waistband. He all but held his breath waiting for her to move because he knew he would catch a glimpse of the creamy white skin of her abdomen. When it happened, his palms tingled and he curled his hands into fists, battling the urge to touch her. It didn't help that she wasn't wearing a bra.

Focus on something else, Riley, he ordered himself.

Raising his gaze, he studied the top of her head. Her red hair was pulled into a ponytail at her crown and spilled curls everywhere. Why that should make him think of summer nights and twisted sheets was a mystery—and damned frustrating. Apparently there was no safe territory where Maggie Benson was concerned.

If his hands weren't fisted already, he would have done it then as he fiercely fought the unrelenting desire to touch her. He could tell she'd taken some time with her appearance. As much as he tried to feel otherwise, he would enjoy the hell out of mussing her—

He swore softly. He was an idiot for not having this conversation over the phone. He was angry as hell at what she'd done to him. But face-to-face, with her all cute and colorful, was making him forget. Damn it, he was a specially trained operative who'd learned to control his emotions. What was it about Maggie and her lie that made him feel so out of control? He'd done some things that he could never be proud of. But he'd always been under orders. What was her excuse?

She had given birth to his child and never told him.

How could he ever forget that? Even after the way she'd kissed him last night. It seemed like a lifetime ago, but, God help him, he wanted her to do it again.

"Why don't we go into the family room?" she suggested.

"That's appropriate. Although you never gave us a chance to be a family."

She visibly winced, but didn't say anything. Turning away, she headed for the other room and he followed. He struggled to ignore her trim back and the soft curves of her bottom—and the way he wanted to explore her from her silky hair to her slender ankles. Why couldn't she have worn jeans? Denim would have better camouflaged her feminine form. It would have been so much easier to resist touching than the smooth thin knit she wore.

"Would you like a beer? Or something stronger?"

"Beer would be fine."

He wanted the something stronger, but any alcohol was a bad move since it was tops on the list of things to never do if you want to keep a clear head. He had the uncomfortable feeling he just wanted to watch her as she walked away from him. She came back into the room and handed him a long-neck.

"Thanks," he said, taking it from her. He was careful to not let his fingers touch hers.

She sat on the sofa, arm's length from a glass of wine that waited on the coffee table. She looked up at him. "Let's get one thing straight right now. Faith *is* your daughter. In case you were wondering."

"I wasn't."

On some level he'd known as soon as he'd met the child. He'd rationalized, justified and finally decided that Maggie must have taken up with another guy right after he'd let her go. Although there was a part of him that never quite believed his own explanation. Maybe because he couldn't understand how a man like him could be responsible for someone as pure, innocent and untainted as Faith. And maybe because he couldn't stand the idea of Maggie with anyone else. How stupid was that?

Faith was *his* child. Even now he couldn't quite take it in. But as soon as Hannah Morgan had pointed out that she had his blue eyes and dark hair with her mother's curls, he'd known it was the truth.

Maggie just looked at him now without speaking. He'd nicknamed her Magpie for a very good reason, but she sure didn't have much to say at the moment. And she definitely had a lot of explaining to do.

"Did you tell her yet?"

She shook her head. "I thought we needed to talk first."

"Let's talk," he prompted. "Why didn't you tell

me about her ten years ago? Why did you keep it a secret?"

She reached for her wineglass and her hand was shaking. Instead of taking a sip, she pulled back and laced her fingers together in her lap. "I planned to tell you—from the moment I could no longer deny the fact that I was pregnant."

"But?"

"I felt it was something I should tell you in person. News like that shouldn't be delivered over the phone or in a letter."

"How sensitive of you," he said. When her eyes darkened, he knew his sarcasm had hit home. "So why didn't you tell me in person?"

"I was waiting until you came home on leave after boot camp."

"And I never came home," he finished.

"On top of that, you dumped me." There was a tinge of anger in her voice and when she met his gaze, her eyes were full of fire.

Why did he suddenly feel as if he were on the defensive? "I still had a right to know," he said.

"Agreed."

"So why didn't I?"

"There was that letter I wrote you. Remember? The one you marked Return to Sender."

If he'd only known. "There were ways to get in touch with me if you'd really wanted to."

"I was a pregnant teenage girl. Put yourself in my shoes."

"Tough assignment."

"Try. You'd just brushed me off with a Dear Jane

letter. Then you refused to read what I had to say. I stopped trying. I was only seventeen."

"Old enough to know what you were doing." He couldn't help another sarcastic jab even though he had a feeling he was digging himself a foxhole he couldn't climb out of.

She pulled her shoulders back and straightened her spine. Pride shone brightly in her eyes. "The worst thing I could imagine was forcing myself and a baby on you, pushing you into something you clearly didn't want. Because I was underage, my parents were threatening legal charges. I didn't want to get you in trouble."

She'd been protecting him? His grandmother was the last person he could remember who'd done that. Soldiers learned to look out for one another, but it was a job. This was personal. He didn't want, need or deserve it.

Jack cranked up his defensive instincts again. He felt the situation slipping away from him and he couldn't let that happen. If he didn't have self-righteous anger, he didn't think there would be anywhere else to take cover. "You never gave me a chance to decide what I wanted."

"I sent you a letter. It's not my fault you dropped off the face of the earth."

A direct hit. When he was involved in a mission, it *was* darn near impossible to get a message to him. That's one of the reasons he hadn't been able to attend his grandmother's funeral. And missing that had been the straw that broke the camel's back. For the umpteenth time he questioned all he'd had to give up to do what he did. For a while now he'd been thinking burnout. He'd ignored the signs. Facing it would mean he'd have to figure out who he was.

Feelings of self-doubt put him on the offensive. "Why should I believe you wrote to let me know about Faith?"

Twin spots of color flared on her cheeks. Her eyes, usually moss-colored, darkened to hunter green. When she stood, he wondered if he'd just pushed the button that would send her into hot-tempered-redhead mode.

"First of all, you were there when she was conceived. But you kept going without looking back. I had to do something."

"I'm not psychic. A guy expects a heads-up for something like that."

"I'll be right back," she snapped.

While she was gone, he looked around the room. On one wall was a frame of collaged photos. He walked over to see them better. There were pictures of Faith from infancy to the present. Some with Maggie and an older couple he assumed were her folks. None of him. He felt a pressure in the center of his chest, near his heart. Anger surged through him again.

And regret for all he'd missed.

When Maggie returned she had an envelope in her hand. She held it out to him and when he took it, she backed away, eyes flashing her own anger. He couldn't help thinking she was beautiful when she was angry.

Then he looked down at the yellowed letter with his boot camp address, instantly recognizing her writing. She'd written him every day and her distinctive scrawl reminded him that she'd been a lonely soldier's link to the world. In the upper left-hand corner was the address where she'd lived with her parents. He'd never been to the house because her folks had decided he was too wild, a bad influence on her. The month and year were clearly marked. Written in his hand across the front was exactly what she'd told him: the directive to Return to Sender.

"Read it," she ordered.

He briefly met her gaze, then turned the still-sealed envelope over. He ripped it open and pulled out a sheet of paper. As he scanned the words, he was very aware of the scared seventeen-year-old she'd been. She wrote that she understood he didn't want to be tied down. But she thought he should know that he was going to be a father and she would always love him. The last words were that she didn't expect anything from him.

And that's exactly what she'd gotten.

He folded the single page, then looked at her. "Maggie, I—"

"You have to understand, Jack. I was practically a baby—having a baby. I did my best. Then I realized I couldn't get in touch with you unless I made a big stink. I didn't want to do that. I decided to move on."

"How?"

"After my parents got over the shock, they were supportive—even when I refused to name the father. After Faith was born, they doted on her. I got my high school equivalency and took some vocational courses at the local college. With a small business loan and some help from Destiny's Sunshine fund, I opened This 'N That. It's been more successful than I ever dreamed. When I realized that my folks were parenting Faith more than I was and we were becoming too dependent on them, I bought this house and moved out."

He watched the shadows that crossed her face and read between the lines. She'd had a rough time of it. He couldn't imagine the strength and courage it had taken to not only get through it but to thrive. Soldiers received medals and commendation for acts of bravery. A Purple Heart for wounds suffered in battle. If the shadows in her eyes were anything to go by, she'd been wounded, too. And he was rubbing salt in it.

"You make it sound easy," he commented.

She shook her head. "It was the hardest thing I've ever done. But it made me strong. I can handle whatever comes my way. I wouldn't change a thing about my life."

"Where are they now? Your parents, I mean."

"Traveling. The Texas summers are hard on them so they get away." She sighed. "Jack, think about it. When I got that letter returned, I never expected to see you again. Why would I think you'd come back to me—to Destiny, I mean?"

"But I did come back. You've had an opportunity or two or ten to tell me the truth." Again, anger coiled inside him like a deadly snake. "I brought it up, then dismissed the idea." He stopped and inhaled a long breath, then looked at her. "I gave you the perfect lead-in. You could have told me. Was that payback?"

"No." She met his gaze. "Again, put yourself in my shoes."

"You're not wearing any." He looked down at her bare feet and hated himself. In spite of the fact that he was irritated as hell, he noticed her pink-painted toenails—and the implied intimacy.

One corner of her full lips tilted up. "Since when are you Mr. Literal? Try to comprehend where I'm coming from."

"Tell me."

She took a deep breath, as if she were about to go

underwater. "I never really knew you. We didn't spend all that much time together ten years ago."

She was right about that. And at least fifty percent of the time they'd shared hadn't been spent talking, he recalled. He and Maggie had been all fire, desire and attraction. They hadn't been able to get enough of each other, and some things didn't change if last night was anything to go by. Leaving her had been the hardest thing he'd ever done. But back then, after a couple brushes with the law, his dad had decided the army would be just the thing to straighten out the wild kid he was becoming. He'd been right.

"Go on," he urged.

"Out of the blue, you walk back into my life with no information except that you're career military. You can't tell me what you've been up to for the last ten years so how could I trust you with the fact that you're Faith's father? My duty, first and foremost, is to protect her."

He couldn't fault her for that. "Okay."

"Is that all you can say?" she cried.

"It's a polite response while I assimilate information."

"Look, Jack." She huffed out a breath, clearly irritated and trying to stay calm. "You said you weren't going to stay in town long. If Faith knew about you, she'd want to spend time with you but you'd be gone again." A look of pain and desolation crossed her face. "She's learned to get along without a father because she had to. Since you weren't going to be around anyway, I wasn't sure rocking the boat was wise."

"But you knew I'd decided to stay—for the time it would take to make sure the house is mine."

"True. But I needed to know what kind of man you are before revealing the truth. Then there was last night when I found you in here." She glanced at the couch, a guilty, nervous look on her face. "The next thing I knew, I was on my back looking at Attila the Hun."

She was right. But for the life of him, he couldn't regret the kiss that had resulted from his soldier's instincts. If the pink in her cheeks was any indication, she hadn't forgotten, either. Did she regret it?

Now was not the time to be distracted by the memory of her sweet lips and even sweeter curves. "Nothing you've said changes the fact that she's my daughter and I had a right to know about her."

"That's true."

"You should have said something right away. You let me believe some guy walked out on you."

"Some guy *did* walk out on me."

He remembered Faith telling him about her father and that she hadn't been abandoned. At least Maggie hadn't trashed him to her. He braced himself for the intoxicating smell of her when she moved beside him and looked up.

"It's not the kind of thing a woman can just blurt out. 'Hi, Jack, how've you been? Oh, by the way, you're a father.'" She looked at him and let him absorb her words. "Besides, there was always the chance that if you knew, you might want to be a part of her life. I needed to know more before I let you in. I couldn't take chances."

She was right to be wary of him. The things he'd seen and done made him feel tainted. But the fact remained—Faith was his child.

He was a father.

Maggie had tried to tell him about the pregnancy. He believed that. As for the rest… Maybe she'd planned to clue him in. Maybe not. But she was a good mother who was doing her level best to be both parents to his daughter. Maggie was trying to protect Faith, even if it meant saving her from him. As much as he wanted to, he couldn't fault her for that, either. If he could change his past and the hard man he'd become, he would do it in a heartbeat. Odd thought. He wasn't sure he had a heart anymore.

Maggie leaned a shoulder against the wall between the kitchen and the family room. She looked up at him. "I think we need to face the fact that neither of us deliberately did anything wrong. It was just circumstances. Now we have to move on."

For all these years his world had narrowed to right versus wrong, black and white. How was he supposed to deal with all these things that stretched the definition of gray area? He felt his self-righteous indignation slipping away.

"I would never do anything to hurt our daughter," he said defensively.

"I think I knew that all along." She met his gaze and her face went soft.

"So what's the plan now?"

She thought for a moment. "It's time to tell Faith that you're her father."

"Okay." He took a deep breath and nodded. "Let's start the training."

She smiled. "There's no training in the world that can prepare you to be a parent. Although self-defense is a good start."

* * *

"You nervous?" Maggie asked him the next morning as they waited for their daughter. She was due home any minute from her sleep-over.

"Do I look nervous?" Jack answered.

He was standing in her kitchen with a cup of coffee in his hand. Maggie studied him. He was wearing jeans that sat easy on his lean hips and molded to his muscular thighs. His black T-shirt clung to every muscle and contour in his torso and arms. His hair was still damp from his morning shower and there wasn't a hint of shadow on his rugged jaw. She could smell the spicy, get-your-heart-rate-up fragrance of his aftershave. Obviously he wanted to make a good impression. And he definitely made an impression on her. He cleaned up real nice and looked sexy as hell. But not nervous.

"Aren't you even a little bit scared?" she asked.

He gave her a wry look. "Maggie, I've jumped out of an airplane with the enemy shooting rocket-propelled grenades past my ear. I've been pinned down by snipers and survived suicide bombings on the other side of the world."

"What was I thinking? Of course you're not scared," she agreed.

"I'm terrified." He let out a long breath.

So he was human, after all. Her heart hurt as regret for what might have been welled up inside her. "Jack, there's something I need to ask you."

"Shoot," he answered, then took a sip of his coffee and met her gaze.

"Are you upset? Or should I say, how upset are you still?" She studied him, the black hair, blue eyes, creases on either side of his nose and mouth. "I—I didn't sleep much last night. And I tried to put myself in your shoes, to figure out what you must be feeling. God knows, you don't give a girl much of a clue."

He leaned a muscular shoulder against the wall that separated her kitchen and dining room. "I didn't sleep much, either," he admitted. "Honestly, I think I'm numb."

"Okay." Her own polite response while she assimilated information. Good technique.

"I'm not sure about anything anymore."

"I can accept that. But are you angry with me?"

"Why are you asking me that now?"

"Because if you are, I was hoping you could put it aside when we talk to Faith. We need to make this as matter-of-fact as possible, she'll accept things more easily."

He nodded. "I'll do my best. But you have to realize that, intellectually, I understand why you did what you did. Then I come up against the fact that my daughter has been around for nine years and I didn't know. That gets to me." He shook his head. "Then I realize I'm a *father.* That blows my mind. It's going to take some time to deal with that reality."

Maggie heard a car door slam. "Well, time is something of a shortage right now. You're up, Ace. She's home."

"Okay. Ready to rock and roll."

Maggie watched his Adam's apple bob up and down as he swallowed. He set his coffee mug on the counter and straightened. Any second, she expected him to salute.

The front door opened then slammed. "Mo-om? I'm home."

"In the kitchen," Maggie called out, then lowered her voice to speak to Jack. "She's going to love you. Just be yourself."

"Why doesn't that make me feel better?" he muttered.

A moment later Faith bounced into the room. "Hi, Mom. Hey, Jack. You having breakfast with Mom? I'm starving. What're we eating?"

"Didn't you eat at Becky's house?" Maggie asked.

"Nope. I didn't like what her mom fixed."

Maggie narrowed her gaze on her offspring. "Did you and Becky get along okay this time?"

Faith flounced into one of the chairs at the table in the nook and gave her the don't-you-know-anything look. "She always wants her way, Mom."

"So that's a no?"

Instead of answering, the child looked at the man she would soon find out was her father. "What are you doing here, Jack?"

Here goes, Maggie thought. Nothing would ever be the same again. The butterflies clog-dancing in her stomach felt as big as bats.

"Jack and I have something to tell you."

Faith looked from one to the other. "You're getting married?" she blurted out.

"No." Maggie glanced at him to see if he'd had any reaction to the remark.

His face hadn't changed. Silly her. The man guarded his emotions as securely as the Secret Service watched over the president. She walked over to the table and sat at a right angle to her daughter. "Do you remember when you used to ask me questions about your father?"

Faith nodded. "Yeah. You said he left town and disappeared before you could tell him about me. But that if he'd known, he would have been here."

"That's right," Maggie confirmed. "Well, I have some good news. Your father has come home."

Faith stared at her, then Jack. Blue eyes so like his grew wide. Maggie could almost see the wheels in her child's head spinning like a slot machine, falling into place as she won the jackpot.

Faith pointed. "It's him? He's my father?"

"That's right." Maggie smiled and nodded.

For several moments there was silence in the room. Maggie had never quite understood the meaning of pregnant silence until now. It seemed somehow fitting since that's what had started this whole thing in the first place.

Jack moved to the table and hunkered down in front of Faith. "Your mom's right. If I'd known about you, I'd have come back as soon as I could. But I didn't know. Your mom tried to get in touch with me. I had some—jobs—that kept me away for a long time."

Maggie could tell he was picking his words carefully. "Your dad is an army hero, Faith."

"Do you have medals?" she asked.

He shrugged and shook his head. "I'm no hero. Just a man. But you need to understand that what happened isn't anyone's fault. Circumstances kept us apart. But I'm here now. And I hope we can spend some time together. Get to know each other."

Maggie held her breath, watching her child's face as she listened to Jack's words. What was she thinking? Feeling? She and Jack were adults and this was a traumatic situation for them. Faith was only nine years old. How would she take this all in?

"Wow." Faith tucked a black curl behind her ear and looked shyly into her father's face. "My very own dad."

"Yeah." One corner of Jack's mouth lifted. "What do you think about that?"

"I think—" She glanced at her mother. "I bet Mom's glad you're here. She always says I'm more than one person can handle."

"Are you?" he asked still looking at his daughter as if she might disappear any second.

"Nah. But Mom will be glad to have you for backup."

"How do *you* feel about it?" Maggie asked, trying to prod her into sharing what was going on inside her. Did her reluctance to talk about things come from her father?

Faith thought for a minute. "I think it's cool. He can come to my softball games. And soccer games. Maybe he can be a coach for my team, like Becky's dad."

"Whoa," Maggie warned. "Let's not go too fast. Remember, Jack's here temporarily. Until G.G. Dot's house is all settled."

"Okay," Faith said. "But while he's here, we can hang out."

"I'd like that, Faith," he said. "So, you're okay with this?"

"Yeah. Wanna play catch with me?"

"Sure."

Thank God for sports, Maggie silently prayed. "Okay then," she said. "But first, how about you take your sleep-over stuff into your room and put it away?"

"O-okay," Faith said.

Jack stood and stared at her. She hopped off the chair

and dramatically dragged herself across the room, to the doorway where she'd dropped her things.

She stopped and turned, glancing at Jack. On her small face was a look filled with such longing it cracked Maggie's heart in two. As if she thought *he* might disappear at any second.

"Jack—I mean, Dad?" she said tentatively. "Is it all right if I call you that?"

"Is that what you want to call me?"

She nodded. "Would it be okay if I gave you a hug?" she asked seriously.

A lump the size of Destiny clogged Maggie's throat, making her forget about how much her heart hurt.

"I could use a hug," Jack answered just as seriously.

He hunkered down and Faith slowly moved closer to him. He waited, almost as if he didn't know what to do. Of course he didn't, Maggie realized. She didn't suppose his way of life allowed for hugs from little girls on a regular basis.

Faith stepped between his widespread knees and put her arms around his neck. Maggie saw his face. If she hadn't known better, she'd have thought he was in pain. But slowly he put his strong arms around their little girl and pressed her as carefully as spun glass against his chest. No one was supposed to hear the small sigh that escaped him when he closed his eyes and buried his face in Faith's hair as she rested her cheek on his shoulder.

Maggie's eyes filled with tears and she put a hand over her mouth as she studied the two dark heads so close together. All the lost years. Guilt flooded her. Could she have done more to find him? Should she have? He'd discovered something he was good at, at a time he'd needed it. But he and Faith had missed out on so much.

Finally the child straightened and moved away from the circle of his arms. She smiled at him. "I hafta go put my stuff away. Then we can play." She started out of the room. "Will you show me how to do some of that kung fu stuff you were doing yesterday?"

"No. But I'd like you to promise me that you won't fall out of the tree again," he said.

"Okay." Then Faith turned, grabbed her backpack and ran from the room.

Maggie let out a long breath. "When she gets back, I'll sidetrack her with food. She needs to eat. So if you've got things to do, don't feel obligated to play catch with her."

"I want to spend time with her," he said. "There's a lot I have to make up for."

Maggie shook her head. "There's nothing to make up for. You said it yourself. It's nobody's fault—just circumstances."

"Still—I want to get to know her."

Here we go, Maggie warned herself. The intimacy of sharing a child with him threatened to pull her in again. And she already knew the danger he posed to her heart.

"And I want you to know her, Jack. But be careful with her. She leads with her emotions and doesn't hold anything back," she warned.

"What does that mean?"

"She's easily hurt." Like mother, like daughter, Maggie thought.

"I wouldn't hurt her."

"Not deliberately. I didn't mean to imply that. But circumstances being what they are—"

"Which is?" he all but growled.

"You're only here until you can secure title to your grandmother's house. After that—you're out of here again. Where does that leave Faith?" And me, she silently added. "She'll get used to spending time with you, then you'll be off to the other side of the world dodging suicide bombers."

Maggie already knew how much it hurt when Jack Riley left. Now that Faith knew the truth about him, they would spend time together. But Maggie would do everything in her power to minimize their daughter's broken heart when he went back to his real life.

"I don't want Faith hurt when you go away."

He rested his hands on his hips and looked down at his boots for several moments. Then he met her gaze. "I've given this a lot of thought."

"Define 'this.'"

"Faith. Me. The whole father/daughter thing."

"And?"

"I plan to resign my commission. I'm staying in Destiny."

Stunned, Maggie couldn't even breathe for several moments. She couldn't believe what he'd said. Although numb, one thing was crystal clear. Ten years ago she'd protected Jack. After Faith was born, all her energy had gone into protecting her child. Now it was time to protect herself. From him.

He'd said he was staying. Maggie knew she couldn't make him go. He outweighed her by a hundred pounds at least. No way could she throw him out of town. But he was sticking around because of his child, not the mother of his child.

He'd broken her heart once. She wouldn't let him do it again. Not without resisting him every step of the way.

Chapter 8

A week after telling Faith that he was her father, Jack pulled his mail from the brick mailbox at the curb. Casually he sifted through the junk envelopes. Then, the same time as usual, he saw Maggie's red compact car turn the corner and head toward him. He noted a hitch in his breathing as anticipation expanded in his chest. Apparently tamping down his emotions in civilian life was going to be harder than he'd thought. Especially when it came to Maggie—and the unbelievably big feelings his daughter had generated in him.

In the past seven days he'd hung out with Faith a lot. Several times her mother had let her skip camp to stay with him while she was at her shop. Then there were the occasions when his daughter had eaten dinner at his house and shown up on his doorstep first thing in the morning. He didn't mind. He had a lot of time to make up for.

His gaze focused on Maggie's car. Their driveways reminded him of mini-runways separated by a narrow grass median. She pulled in and stopped her small car even with where he parked his black sport utility vehicle. As he'd done for the past week, he waited for his anger toward her to surface and wasn't completely surprised when it didn't. She hadn't put up a single hurdle in his mission to get to know his daughter. Why shouldn't he let go of the past and move forward?

Besides, he had more important ways to spend his energy. Like being a parent. There was no doubt in his mind that it was the hardest yet most important job he would ever do. But no pressure, he thought wryly.

Maggie got out of her car and waved. He envied the way she handled mothering Faith. She made setting limits look simple. She easily walked the walk and talked the talk while he felt as if he'd just stumbled naked into a minefield. His training for this op was nonexistent.

He raised his hand to return her greeting. Something compelled him to speak. "What are you doing home at this hour?" As if he didn't know.

She met him in his yard. "I always come home for lunch around this time."

He would be lying if he said he wasn't glad to see her. That feeling was responsible for the next words that came out of his mouth.

"I just ordered a pizza. Want to join me?" he asked. Please say yes, he thought. He found he very much wanted to spend time with her. Alone.

She raised her sunglasses and rested them on her head, studying him intently. Moving forward, she put her hand on his forehead as if checking for fever. "You okay?"

He savored the touch of her small, cool hand and tried to ignore the way his heart lurched. "Why?"

She shrugged. "Just checking. Thought maybe you were delirious or something."

"Why would you think that?"

"It seems out of character for you to make social nice."

"Then maybe it's time to change that. Do you want some pizza or not?"

"Do I have 'stupid' written on my forehead? Pizza sounds great. Especially compared to the peanut butter and jelly sandwich I was planning on," she said smiling.

He was dazzled by the look she sent him. Saucy, sassy and full of sunshine. An almost-overwhelming urge to pull her into his arms churned inside him. Instead of acting on it, he turned away. "Follow me," he said.

He led the way and stopped just inside his door, letting his eyes adjust from the glare in the yard. It was cool after the noon heat outside. He took notice of the formfitting denim sundress she wore and the way it outlined her curvy little figure to perfection. Her slender arms and the part of her shoulders he could see were sprinkled with freckles. He remembered that she hated them, but he thought they were cute. He wouldn't change them even if he had the power.

Maggie set her purse on the hall tree resting against the long entry wall. "It's a hot one today," she commented.

"Yeah." And getting hotter by the second, thanks to his big mouth. "Can I get you a soda?"

"Do you have anything diet?" she asked.

"Because you don't want to sabotage your low-fat pizza experience?" he asked, unable to keep from smiling.

"A girl needs to save a calorie wherever she can." She followed him into the kitchen. "Does that mean you don't have anything diet?"

"Yeah. How about sweet tea?"

"Sounds great." She looked around the room while he pulled the pitcher from the fridge. "It looks the same as it did when your grandmother was here."

He heard the sadness in her voice as he set the glasses and pitcher of tea on the center island. "You miss her, don't you?"

She nodded and blinked at the sudden sheen of moisture in her eyes. "She was like family." Laughing shakily, she added, "I guess she actually was family, at least to my daughter. Our daughter," she amended. "I wish she'd known you were Faith's father."

"Me, too." When the doorbell rang he said, "Chow's here."

He went and paid the delivery guy, giving him a generous tip. Then he took the cardboard box and carried it to the kitchen. While he'd been occupied, Maggie had found plates, utensils and napkins and set them out on the oak table occupying the cozy nook. She waited by one of the four ladderback chairs.

"Lunch is served," he said, placing the box on the table.

She breathed deeply. "Smells wonderful. Mushroom and black olive, I bet."

"You can smell that?"

"I didn't have to. It's your favorite."

He couldn't believe she remembered. Then he recalled that she used to kid him about being a closet vegetarian and what would the guys say if she blew his cover. He missed those carefree days, before his job had turned him cynical and suspicious. He'd once taken pride in his ability to perform his duties with exemplary skill. Now he just felt stripped of his humanity—always expecting the worst.

"Have a seat. I'll get the drinks," he said gruffly.

When he brought them back to the table, she'd already put several pieces of pizza on his plate and a slice on her own.

"This is great," she said, taking a bite. "Almost as great as what you were doing on the computer."

He glanced at his system set up on the built-in desk in the corner of the kitchen. His house, or rather his grandmother's, was almost a duplicate of Maggie's. The two tract homes had identical floor plans, but flip-flopped. In the excitement of seeing her while getting his mail, he'd forgotten about the research he'd been doing on the Internet.

"What about what I was doing?" he asked.

"You were reading up on parenting," she accused.

"And why would you think that?"

"I can read. I saw the sites you were searching. 'Spare the Rod, Spoil the Child.' 'Discipline and Love'—not necessarily in that order—'A Parent's Tools.' 'Dads and Daughters—A Special Bond.' It doesn't take a mental giant to figure out what you're up to."

He rubbed a hand across the back of his neck. "Guilty as charged."

She held her slice of pizza and stopped halfway to her mouth. "To research parenting techniques on the

Internet. How sweet is that? Guilty is not the word I would choose. Something tells me when you discovered computers you found a friend. And you're pumping him for information. I think it's great."

"I'm not sure whether to say thank you, or if them's fightin' words." He shrugged to hide his pleasure at her praise. "I feel like I've walked into a movie that has already started and I'm playing catch-up."

"Oh, Jack—"

He reached across the table and touched her hand. Electricity zinged up his arm and he quickly pulled back. "It was just an observation, not a criticism."

"You're not angry?" she asked, an intense expression on her face, as if his answer meant a lot to her.

"Not now."

She brushed a napkin across her impossibly lush lips. "How could I have ever thought you were dangerous?"

"Because I am."

She made a sound that was an awful lot like an unladylike snort. "About as dangerous as a teddy bear. Somehow I'm going to find a way to convince you of that."

"Good luck. In polite society, I'm a hazard."

"The only hazard I can see," she said, chewing thoughtfully, "is to my heart."

"What?"

She went completely still, then swallowed hard, as if she'd bitten off more than she could chew. "What I meant was, and this isn't an easy thing to admit—"

"Go on," he prodded, his own heart racing as if he'd just run a 10K. Was she saying what he thought? Or were his social skills as nonexistent as he believed?

"That fact is—"

"What, Maggie? Spit it out."

"It's not very attractive of me. And I'm not very proud of the feeling."

"C'mon. This is me."

"Yeah. You. The father Faith has just found. The truth is I'm jealous of you and your relationship with her."

He let out the breath he hadn't realized he was holding. Why would he have thought she was going to say her heart was in danger from him? Because she cared about him? Instead of resigning his commission in the army, he should have been drummed out on a Section Eight—mental problems. "You're joking."

"I wish I were. For the past week I've hardly seen her. She wants to spend every waking moment with you."

"Have I thanked you for letting her spend as much time with me as you have?"

"Yes. And I feel the need to confess that if you hadn't invited me for pizza, I'd have been knocking on your door, anyway. She forgot her baseball mitt."

"I could have taken the glove to her at camp."

"I know. That's my point. I needed her to need me." She sighed. "In defense of my shallowness I feel compelled to point out that since she was born, I've been everything to her. And now here you are."

This time he couldn't help it. He grinned from ear to ear. "I'm not sure whether to say thank you or 'I'm sorry' and 'It won't happen again.'"

"I'm not asking you to do either. This is my problem. I need to deal with it. Suddenly I feel as if I don't fit anywhere. On top of that, I'm competing with a hero."

"I think we covered this already. I'm no hero."

"As far as Faith is concerned you are. You can do no

wrong. In fact she's convinced you're going to propose to me."

"Marriage?" Jack almost choked on his tea. He swallowed and coughed, then said, "She is?"

Maggie nodded, then pointed a warning finger at him. "Don't even think about it."

"Why would I?"

Other than the obvious reasons that she was gorgeous, gutsy and he couldn't get her out of his mind. But he had no intention of inflicting himself on Maggie and Faith, except in an auxiliary capacity. They deserved a better man than him in their lives.

"You would because you're a good man. Noble." She wagged a finger at him. "You've got to watch that. Just because we share a child doesn't mean we have to get married. Two wrongs don't make a right."

"It isn't wrong if two people love each other." Whoa. For a guy with no heart, he had a hell of a nerve spouting relationship counsel.

"True. But that's the only reason for getting married. When you think about it, we hardly know each other. We've been apart longer than we've ever been together. The sequence of events in our lives is completely out of whack. It wouldn't work."

Jack wanted to argue that she was wrong. If they wanted it badly enough, they could make it work. Then he remembered who he was and the things he'd done and realized he had no business arguing anything. He would consider himself lucky if he could spend time with his daughter and not have any of the dirtiness that was his life rub off on her.

"Why haven't you ever married?" he asked. "Because of Faith?"

"Partly," she admitted. "No one can love her the way I—" shyly she met his gaze "—I mean, you and I—no one can love her that way. I didn't want to trap her in a situation she had no control over." She picked at her pizza crust. "Do you believe in soul mates?" she asked, studying him.

"I don't know—"

She laughed at him. "You could look more uncomfortable, but I'm not sure how. The other reason I never took the plunge is that I haven't met anyone who felt like—"

"What?" he asked, the blood pounding through his veins. He wanted her to say she hadn't met anyone like him.

Maggie took a deep breath, horrified at what she'd almost revealed. She'd almost said she hadn't met anyone like him. True, he was the only man who had ever touched her soul. It was also too true that she had a bad feeling he was the only one who ever *could* touch her, at least the way he had ten years ago. But now she sensed he wouldn't reach out again. Or worse, believed he couldn't.

"Tell me again why you never told anyone I'm Faith's father."

She shrugged. "I overheard your father bragging about you. He said you'd found your niche in the army and were doing great. I didn't want to blow that for you."

"So you kept quiet and went through childbirth and raising Faith alone. And did a damn fine job."

"I had my parents."

"The same ones you kept a secret from. To protect me. Who's really the hero, Maggie?"

The intense expression in his vivid blue eyes took her breath away. "I was scared to death. But I just did what I had to." The words were barely more than a whisper past the lump in her throat and her hammering heart.

"Isn't that what a hero does? What he—or she—has to do in spite of the fear?"

"She's my child. I love her. It's not a big deal."

"You're wrong. It is a big deal. And I—"

"What?" she prompted, hoping.

"I admire you very much," he finished.

That was almost as good as love. Right? It wasn't the can't-wait-to-see-you, I-hurt-when-I'm-not-with-you kind of feelings they'd had when they were teenagers. But it was something.

She had no right to wish or to expect anything from him—not for herself. She hadn't wanted to force him into that ten years ago. And she still felt the same way. Somehow she would have to find the courage to reconcile herself to the reality of her situation.

She'd come to terms with the fact that she'd created reasons to hold back the truth from him. It was one thing for him to leave after high school, to discover and build a new life. It was something else for him to stay in Destiny and turn his back on her because he just couldn't care about her the way she wanted him to. That was just too pitiful. Not a good enough reason to withhold the truth, but she'd already admitted to him that she was shallow. She didn't have to confess this out loud, too, did she?

She stood. "Thanks for the pizza, Jack. It's getting late and I have to get back to the shop. If you could get Faith's mitt for me, I'll run it over to her at camp."

He stood, too. "Are you sure you don't want me to do that?"

"No. I have to go out anyway."

He nodded. "Okay."

He disappeared and returned several moments later with the baseball glove. "Here."

She took it, carefully avoiding the touch of his warm, strong fingers. "Thanks. By the way, Mr. Internet," she said. "I noticed that the computer store in town is up for sale."

"Oh?"

She nodded. "Have you figured out yet what you want to be when you grow up?"

"Meaning I have too much time on my hands since leaving the military?"

"If the combat boot fits..." She shrugged. "Anyway, I thought you might be interested. See you later."

"I hope so."

Hope. She turned quickly away before he could see tears in her eyes that she couldn't control. Her hopes were so much bigger than all those years ago yet so incredibly hopeless. Her heart hurt just thinking about it.

Several days later Maggie's heartache hadn't improved. If anything, she was going downhill fast and couldn't seem to slow her descent. Glancing out in her backyard, the reason for her decline played catch with her—correction, *their*—daughter. Faith had insisted her father come over for dinner. Other than the danger to her own heart, Maggie couldn't come up with an excuse to say no. He'd joined them for hamburgers, even done the grilling as if he'd spent the past ten years setting domestic standards in the suburbs.

Instead of joining them in the yard, which Maggie

had been sorely tempted to do, she was cleaning the kitchen. And the whole quirky scene felt like something out of a whacked-out sitcom.

Jack laughed at something Faith said, and Maggie glanced over her shoulder and out the screen door. The smile on his face made her want to march right out there and wrap her arms around his waist, snuggling against his rather impressive chest. His blue eyes and devilish grin made her feel as if he'd tossed a lasso around her and was tugging her toward him.

Turning away from the tempting sight, she sprinkled cleanser in her sink and started to scrub as if her life depended on perfectly pristine porcelain. When there was nothing left to cleanse, mop, scour, sweep or wash, she was forced to find something else to keep her indoors and away from the call to danger. She and Jack shared a child, but that didn't mean they would share a life—as in a man/woman sort of thing. Because of Faith she was forced to see him. But that didn't mean she could hang out with them, not if she wanted to keep what was left of her heart in one functional piece.

She poured herself an iced tea and grabbed the newspaper, spreading it out on the table. Outside, she could hear Faith talking. Father and daughter had abandoned their game of catch and were sitting side by side on the glider swing on the patio, in her direct line of vision. Tomorrow Maggie planned to move the swing up against the house where she couldn't see it. Just in case this after-dinner-hanging-out-time became a tradition.

"He's such a dork."

"Who?" Jack asked.

"Logan Peterson."

"Isn't he the one who was tormenting you the day you came home from camp by yourself?"

"That's him," Faith confirmed.

"So what's he done now?"

Maggie would like to know the answer to that, too.

"He hides and when I walk by he pushes me. He calls me names. Pulls my hair, that kind of stuff. I wish you'd show me how to do some of those kung fu kicks and stuff," Faith said.

"We talked about this, kiddo. I do it for exercise."

"But he won't leave me alone," Faith complained.

"The little creep—"

Maggie heard the menace in Jack's voice. He joked about knowing three hundred ways to kill with his bare hands, but surely he drew the line at children—no matter how big a dork Logan Peterson happened to be.

"Yeah, he's a real turkey," Faith agreed.

"I've got an idea," Jack said. "How about if I take you to camp tomorrow. While I'm there, I can warn the little jerk to leave you alone."

"Cool," their child said enthusiastically.

Not cool, Maggie thought.

She stood and opened the slider. "Faith, it's time for you to take your bath and get ready for bed."

Jack looked at Maggie through the red haze of his anger. The last six weeks in Destiny had opened him up to assaults on his senses from every direction. He prided himself on his ability to remain cool and in control. Yet Maggie and Faith tapped into his dormant emotions, which led into the colors that continually bombarded him. He took a deep breath.

"Mo-om, it's too early for bathtime," she protested.

"No, it's not. Remember, you owe me a half hour

because you stayed up late last night to finish watching that video with your dad."

Your dad.

The words still caught Jack up short. He was someone's father. He had a little girl. And some little so-and-so was picking on her. It made him see red all over again.

"Dad, I'm nine. Tell her it's too early for me to get ready for bed."

He looked at the mutinous expression on the child's face. "Your mom is the ranking officer. You did promise to hit the rack earlier tonight if you could stay up later last night."

"I can't believe you're on her side," Faith protested.

"I'm on your side, believe it or not. I think you've been given a direct order. Time to carry it out. On the double."

He watched the girl dramatically drag herself to the house and shoot her mother a drop-dead look before she disappeared inside. Maggie called some directions to the child, then closed the sliding door and walked toward him. She was in shorts, crop top and bare feet—just about the most blatantly sexy look she could possibly have, short of wearing nothing at all.

He held his breath, alternately hoping she would sit beside him and praying she wouldn't. She didn't.

Standing in front of him, she rested her fists on her hips. "Jack, we need to talk."

Words every man dreaded.

"Okay. What about?"

"I overheard what Faith told you about Logan Peterson," she said.

Just the name twisted his gut into an angry knot. "The little creep needs a good talking to—"

"No."

He blinked at her and stood. "Excuse me?"

"I said you can't talk to him."

"Why not?"

"Sometimes being a parent means doing nothing."

"Not when some boy is pulling my daughter's hair."

Maggie sighed, a big gusty breath of air. "I know it's hard. But you and I won't always be here to run interference. She's got to learn to handle things on her own."

"Maggie, I'll admit I'm new at this father thing." He saw her face cloud. "That wasn't a criticism, just a fact. I am new." He rubbed a hand across the back of his neck. "But I gotta tell you, I'd give my life for that child."

"I know how you feel," she said, then caught the corner of her bottom lip between her teeth. "But there are times when backing off is the best course of action. She needs to learn to handle whatever life throws at her. Training starts now. If you butt in, she won't get a chance to flex those problem-solving muscles."

"Intellectually I understand what you're telling me. But in my gut, I want to make her world perfect."

"Believe me, I'd like to take the little jerk aside and give him a tongue-lashing he wouldn't forget anytime soon. And there are times when you have to step in, as far as alerting the adults around her about what's going on. But in the meantime, let's see what happens. Maybe it will blow over."

"Maybe." But he didn't really buy that. His gut was telling him to fix it.

"I suspect he's trying to get her attention. Wouldn't

surprise me if he's got a crush on Faith," Maggie said, a slight smile turning up the corners of her full lips.

"Yeah, well he's got a funny way of showing it."

He looked down at Maggie, the gathering shadows stealing the color from her hair. She was small and delicate in spite of her spirit and fire. He found he wanted to gather her to him and keep her safe, too. She'd had a hard time of it, thanks to him. But he was here now. For better or worse.

At the same time he wanted to protect Maggie, he found her incredibly sexy and appealing. She was on his mind day and night. Every time he saw her, he had to fight the urge to put his hands on her and explore all the soft, sweet curves he remembered from a decade ago.

"Fathers protect their little girls," he said gruffly.

"Yes, and she's lucky to have a father like you."

Jack was the lucky one. He was incredibly fortunate to share a child with a woman as special as Maggie. Fatherhood was an op he'd all but given up on.

Did he feel more for her than just a man and woman who shared a child? Was it love?

The thought shook him to his core.

"You should go in and check on her," he suggested. "And it's time for me to go."

Twisting her fingers together, she looked down, then glanced up and met his gaze. "Don't feel bad, Jack. I didn't mean to rain on your parade—as far as taking Logan down. It's just—I've been dealing with it a little longer than you have."

"Yeah."

He turned and walked away, letting himself out the side gate. Was it okay? Would anything ever be again?

Faith was his child—his flesh and blood. He was her father. Although she hadn't won the lottery with him, nothing could change that fact. He would deal with the situation and do his best to take care of her. He loved her—hard as it was for him to believe himself capable of the emotion.

But what about Maggie?

Up until now his life had been all about control. He'd suppressed his emotions to complete the mission—whatever it took. He was cynical and looked for the worst in people. Maggie deserved someone uncontaminated, uncorrupted. Loving his child was one thing. He didn't think he was capable of feelings for a woman that were bright, wholesome and unsullied.

This time her parents didn't have to forbid him to see Maggie. He would stay away—for her sake.

Chapter 9

It was Sunday, a day of rest.

Thank God, Maggie prayed, not missing the irony. Her store was closed on Sundays—no exceptions. She was off. After pouring herself a cup of coffee, she quietly opened both the sliding-glass and screened doors, then let herself onto the patio. Faith was still asleep.

Maggie liked to get up early, especially on Sunday. It was her time. No one needed anything from her or pulled her in ten different directions. When she attended church later with Faith, God didn't care whether or not she had on makeup. Her clothes weren't important. Although she couldn't go like she was now—cut-off sweatpants, baggy T-shirt, no bra, barefoot.

Standing on the patio, she enjoyed the breeze that brushed the hair back from her temples like a lover's hands. It was downtime like this that she treasured. She could think. About anything she wanted.

Right now the first thing that came to her mind was Jack—an altogether sexy and seductive thought. A vision jumped into her mind—Jack in worn jeans that fit him like a second skin and a black T-shirt that conformed to each and every incredibly masculine contour in his broad chest and muscled arms. When her breathing instantly quickened, she was grateful to be alone.

"Hi, Maggie."

Startled, she dropped her mug, shattering it on the cement. The liquid splashed on her bare legs. "Jack!" she cried.

In two strides he was beside her, lifting her into his arms without a word. She was too surprised to say anything. His boots crunched on the shards of her mug as he carried her to the edge of the patio and grass where the hose was neatly coiled. Grabbing it, he rinsed off her legs. The cool water felt lovely.

"You okay?" He examined the red blotches on her shins.

"Yeah. No major damage," she said, checking out her own skin. Then she met his gaze. "You gotta quit sneaking up on me like that."

"Sorry. I thought you heard the gate open."

"No."

Heat crept into her cheeks because sexy thoughts of him were the reason she hadn't heard anything and he'd been able to sneak up on her. The deep timbre of his voice raised goose bumps on her arms that spread to her breasts and shoulders. Noting his worn jeans and snug T-shirt, she barely held in a sigh. Jack in the flesh was so much more wonderful than anything her imagination created. The scent of his aftershave, his strength when he'd lifted her into his arms, the warmth of his body so close to hers. Her fantasies didn't do justice to the data her five senses could provide. Sight, sound, smell, touch. The only unstimulated sense was taste.

She could remedy that. All she had to do was stand on tiptoe and touch her mouth to his. Suddenly it seemed like forever since they'd been together on her couch. She remembered her exhilaration when she'd felt the evidence of his desire and known beyond a shadow of a doubt—Jack Riley had wanted her. Deep disappointment and a profound emptiness opened up inside her as she realized it was the last time anything intimate had passed between them.

He'd said he wasn't angry with her for not telling him about Faith sooner. Was he lying?

"Maybe I should put some cream on your legs," he suggested, still checking her out.

"No," she answered just a little too quickly and vehemently.

"Okay." There was the slightest hint of a question in that one word.

As much as she might want any excuse to let him run his hands over her legs, no way could she permit it. Regretting lack of intimacy was one thing; changing it was not smart. She couldn't think of anything more personal than letting him rub lotion on her legs.

Well, that wasn't technically true. She could think of *one* thing that would bring them closer. In fact she remembered like it was yesterday the way he'd climbed through her bedroom window and sneaked into her room ten years ago. The things he'd done and made her feel were forever branded on her memory.

They said everything was bigger in Texas. As far as idiots, she didn't want to be the standard for the Lone

Star State. Letting Jack Riley into her heart a second time would be Texas-size dumb.

She huffed out a big breath. “That's the second time you've scared the living daylights out of me. Actually the third, but it's only the second time I lost coffee over it.”

“You're keeping score?”

She was when the second time she'd wound up flat on her back with Jack on her front and mouth-to-mouth resuscitation not far behind.

“I am. At least this time there's no electronic equipment nearby to short out.” Just my emotions to zap. “From now on maybe you could say ‘hey’, or give me some kind of heads-up?” She backed away from him as the breeze picked up slightly and dried the water on her legs.

“I suppose I could give you some warning.”

“You think?”

He grinned. She noticed he was doing a lot more of that lately and it made her ridiculously happy.

“I need to get a broom to sweep up the glass from my cup,” she said.

“Since I'm technically responsible, I'll do it. In a minute,” he said. “There's something I'd like to talk to you about. To ask you.”

He looked so serious and so darn cute she would have given him anything. “Okay.”

“Have you got any more coffee?” he asked.

“So, it's a coffee kind of chat?”

“No. I just like yours better than mine. And the least I can do is pour you a fresh cup.”

“You've got a point. Yeah, I've got almost a full pot. Let me get you—”

He shook his head. “I didn't rescue you from the

broken mug so you could walk through it on my account. Sit down and I'll get it."

"You've got yourself a deal," she said, lowering herself into the chair.

He disappeared inside and Maggie noticed the acute sense of aloneness that settled over her. Silly because he was coming right back. Second, a nervous sensation took hold. What he wanted to talk about probably had to be about Faith. What did he want to ask?

A proposal? She wasn't sure why that thought popped into her head. Wishful thinking? Not really a stretch because in spite of what he believed, she felt in her gut that he was a man who tried to do the right thing. Did he think the right thing was to marry for the sake of their daughter?

The sliding screened door whispered open. He carried out two mugs, set them down on the small wrought-iron table beside her, then went back to close the door.

"Thanks," she said as he sat in the chair beside hers. Only that small table separated them, and the distance wasn't enough to keep the fresh, clean masculine smell of him from doing funny things to her insides. "So what is it you want to ask?"

"I've been thinking."

"Uh-oh. There's a dangerous prospect."

"Yeah. I'll try to watch it." He blew on his coffee, then took a sip. "But you don't know the half of it. I've been thinking about legal stuff."

"Okay." She studied his profile as she struggled to control her pounding heart. She'd never considered herself especially intuitive and definitely not psychic. But maybe she'd been right. Was he going to ask her to marry him?

"Define 'legal stuff,'" she said cautiously.

"I'm Faith's father."

"And?" she prompted.

"I want to be a part of her life."

"You already are. She adores you."

"I mean legally." He met her gaze. "I want to adopt her. There shouldn't be any doubt about who her father is. I want it spelled out."

"Are you talking about joint custody?"

"I guess I am," he admitted.

Maggie felt like a deflating balloon. To think he would ask her to marry him—Texas-size dumb. Stupid thought; even stupider to care. He just didn't feel that way about her.

"Say something. Even if you think it's a ridiculous idea. A guy like me—"

"No. I'd never think that," she said, reaching out to touch his arm. The skin was warm and dusted with a sprinkling of hair that tickled her fingers. "I don't know what happened to convince you that you're a bad guy with nothing to offer her."

"I don't want to talk—"

"I'm not asking you to tell me. It was merely an observation. I've watched you since you found out the truth—before even. You've taken to fatherhood the way an armadillo takes to underbrush."

One corner of his mouth lifted. "Now that's a flattering analogy."

"I mean it. You spend time with her. Your patience teaching her about the computer is unbelievable. You even saw through her attempts to pit one of us against the other—without coaching from me. She couldn't ask for a better father than you."

"Yeah, she could."

"I'm not going to argue with you about it."

"Okay. So what do you think?"

The only time in her life when she'd been more scared was when she'd discovered she was pregnant with his child and he'd disappeared. That's what she thought. She'd been head over heels in love with him then, with no chance they could be together. That's what she thought, too. But Jack and Faith were father and daughter. A total stranger had figured it out. Even if she wanted, she couldn't deny him his child. So she was facing letting him into her life—really letting him in. Making it legal somehow made it even more real. That's what she thought.

"Maggie?"

She met his gaze and forced a smile to her lips. "I think it's important for Faith to feel secure with a mother and a father."

"So that's a yes?"

"I'll find a lawyer," she answered.

"Jensen Stevens has leased office space in town, right next to the sheriff's office."

"I'll stop by and see her tomorrow and make an appointment for us. Before I open the shop."

"Great."

Yeah, great, she thought. They would be a family—on paper. But she'd never felt further from him. And never wished more fervently it wasn't so.

A week later Maggie was still stewing, a habit-in-the-making since Jack Riley had returned to Destiny. How did she stew?

"Let me count the ways," she muttered.

There were the long sleepless nights. Then she either lost her appetite or was downing junk food as if it was all that stood between her and starvation. If that wasn't bad enough, she zoned out at the worst times and had the concentration of a gnat. All thanks to Wild Jack Riley.

After checking on Faith who was sound asleep, another long, lonely night stretched in front of Maggie. She glanced at the pantry and tried to remember if she'd eaten all the chips, or if there was one last ice-cream sandwich left in the freezer. Before she could find out for sure, she walked onto the patio. Next door, the back spotlight was on in Jack's yard. She knew now it meant he was outside.

The temptation was too much to resist. Maggie peeked at him through the crack in the fence between their houses and felt very much like a little girl—like their daughter who earlier had watched him do his self-defense moves for exercise.

Faith observed him every night. She didn't walk around the house any more like a normal kid. She kicked and waved her arms through the air. Maggie had thought about reprimanding her, but felt it was pretty harmless. Sooner or later her daughter would get over it.

Unlike herself. Maggie peeked through the fence again and lusted after Jack, who was just placing the sprinkler on the grass. How juvenile was her behavior? And she was supposed to guide a child on the straight and narrow? Who thought up this system?

One way or another Maggie knew she was going to have to get a handle on this lusting thing. Letting it continue might be okay as long as there was a chance Jack returned the feeling. After that night of necking on her couch, she'd been so sure he wanted her, too. But ever since finding out Faith was his daughter, the most he'd done was invite her for pizza and keep his hands to himself. A perfect gentleman. A perfectly emotionless robot.

How frustrating was that?

Maggie needed to know whether or not he wanted her. She could keep her heart from harm, especially if she proved once and for all that Jack Riley was indifferent to her. Except as the mother of his daughter.

She placed one sneakered foot on the trunk of the tree in her backyard and started to climb. In several moves she reached the long, sturdy branch that stretched over into his yard. After planting her backside on the branch, she slid across it to his side of the six-foot fence and held on to the limb above her head to keep from falling.

The night was warm. He'd watered his yard and she could smell the moisture and the scent of perfumed flowers that his grandmother had taken such pride in. Interesting that such a dangerous guy went above and beyond the call of duty to preserve them, she thought wryly.

She watched him, hands on his hips with his back to her as he studied the sprinkler pattern to make sure all the plants were watered. Maggie's heart hammered and heat flashed through her that had nothing to do with the warm night. She was playing with fire. She knew it and couldn't stop to save her soul. In his uniform snug jeans and white T-shirt, Jack looked as if he could take on the world, his shoulders seemed a mile wide. Only the state of Texas was big enough for a man like him, she thought, sighing like the seventeen-year-old she'd been the first time she fell in love with him. His black hair curled slightly on his neck, no longer severely military-short. At this moment in time it seemed the most important thing in the world for her to run her fingers through the strands and feel the difference.

Maggie was just about to announce her presence when he said without turning, "You know, everything I saw on the Internet about parenting said you should lead by example. About tree climbing—" He turned around and his teeth flashed white, revealing the grin on his face. "How are you going to tell Faith to do as you say, not as you do?"

"Unless you rat me out, she'll never know."

"She's asleep?" he asked.

"Soundly," Maggie confirmed.

"So what are you doing up in the tree?"

She shrugged. "Impulse action."

"Impulses can get you in a lot of trouble." His voice was soft, subdued, sexy.

The deep, seductive sound jackhammered inside her until Maggie felt the vibrations all the way to her bones. "I don't think it's a problem—unless I fall."

"We can't have that," he said, moving to where she perched.

He gazed up at her, his expression intense, unreadable. He lifted up his hands and put them at her waist. Breathless, Maggie let go of the branch above her and put her palms on a far more secure, not to mention mouth-watering brace—his shoulders.

The muscles there bunched as he easily plucked her from the branch, then let the momentum of her body slide down the front of him. Below her cut-off denims, her bare thighs, knees and shins brushed up against his strength, covered by the soft worn material of his pants. The bottom dropped right out of her stomach. Who needed skydiving for kicks? She could get the same adrenaline rush in Jack Riley's arms.

This had to stop, she decided.

The first time they'd met there had been enough chemistry between them to blow Destiny to kingdom come. With chemistry, a little of this and a bit of that merged to make magic. That's what they'd had. Did they still? Or was it just testosterone and estrogen commingled to make biology? Physiology? Or some other "ology"?

Redheads were not notorious for their passive patience. With every ounce of her being Maggie needed to know where she stood with Jack—emotionally speaking. At the moment she stood with her palms on his shoulders, his hands at her waist, looking into the handsome face that had launched her on this mission in the first place. She might never get a better opportunity to find out if he cared.

Before she could think it to death, she stood on tiptoe and touched her mouth to his. His lips were firm and unyielding—and tasted of surprise.

He broke off the kiss. "Maggie, I— This isn't a good idea—"

But he didn't let her go; he continued to hold her. His gaze was rife with intensity and need. She was certain of it. She nestled closer, as close as she could get with her clothes still on.

"I think it's a great idea," she murmured.

Raising up again, she kissed him. He went still for half a heartbeat, then took command so fast it made her head spin. He wrapped his arms around her, pressing her body more firmly against him, until her breasts flattened against his chest. Hunching his shoulders slightly, he seemed to surround her, protect her. Although it felt like stepping into an emotional vortex, she'd never felt safer or more secure in her life.

He nibbled the corner of her bottom lip, then traced the outline of her mouth until she opened for him. Without hesitation, he plunged inside, testing and teasing as he went. Her breathing grew ragged, shallow. His was a glorious match. She was hot all over yet everywhere he touched tingles started. With one arm securely around her waist, he moved his other hand to cup the back of her head, making the connection of their mouths more firm.

In a sensuous haze she prayed would never clear, Maggie let him have his way with her. He kissed and caressed a path across her cheek to her ear where he captured the lobe between his teeth and gently nipped. Moving just a fraction, he lavished his intensity on the sensitive indentation just below her ear. Suddenly every tingle turned to a chill—of sheer pleasure. A moan rose in her throat. She could no more hold it back than make herself voluntarily stop kissing Jack.

"Maggie," he said in a ragged whisper.

His breath stirred the hair by her ear, tickling, teasing and raising tingles that raced down her spine.

She let out a long breath. "Yes?"

"What you do to me—" He held her against his chest.

Her cheek was pressed to his heart and she swore the pounding was audible. He was warm and strong and so solid she never wanted to leave.

"I was afraid you didn't want me," she confessed. "You haven't kissed me since that night on my sofa when I went head over heels. Literally," she finished with a shaky laugh. His hands, caressing her back in a mesmerizing, seductive movement, suddenly stilled. An awful feeling stole over her. She'd said something and whatever it was, she wanted it back. Pronto.

"Maggie, I—" He took her upper arms in his hands to hold her in place, then moved a step back from her.

"What?"

"This wasn't such a good idea after all."

"Says who? As ideas go, it was great. From my point of view," she said, desperately hoping he shared her point of view.

"I'd only hurt you. Trust me on this."

"You should let me be the judge of that. I know what I'm doing. I'm a big girl—"

"I'm sorry, Mags. I got carried away. But it's not going to work." He dragged in a breath then let it out on a sigh. "Good night, Maggie. I'll see you at Jensen's office tomorrow."

He turned and walked into the house.

Tears burned at the backs of her eyes as she stared for a long moment at the spot where he'd stood warm and solid. Then, in full retreat, she opened his gate and went through it, back to her own yard. Her sanctuary from the cold, brutal truth.

Jack Riley didn't want her.

It hit her suddenly and with crystal clarity. She'd hesitated to tell him about their daughter because she'd been afraid to find out the magic was dead. Instinctively she'd known he was a good man. He'd walked away from her once but that was explainable: they were young, he found a career, she couldn't find him, et cetera. But he was back now—no barriers, no excuses. And he'd just walked away again.

She'd tried to mix hormones and it blew up in her face. They had no chemistry. Correction: he had no chemistry with her. She had enough to light up downtown Destiny during the holiday season.

Damn her stubborn, redheaded impetuousness. Damn her for needing to know. He'd kissed her. He'd stolen the breath from her lungs and made her toes curl. Then as easy as you please, he'd turned his back and walked away. She'd been afraid of this. She wasn't the same person she'd been ten years ago. That girl had been exciting. She'd sneaked around to meet him, against her parents' wishes. Since then, he'd been all over the world, doing heroic things. She was a woman with a child and responsibilities. Pretty unexciting for a guy who ate adventure for breakfast.

"I just have to face facts," she said to herself.

She had feelings—not love, just feelings—for a man who couldn't return them. How stupid was that?

But at least she was experienced in the art of forgetting Jack Riley. She'd done it ten years ago and she would do it now.

Or die trying.

Chapter 10

Jack walked out his front door and saw Maggie unlock her car. It was thirty minutes until they met with Jensen Stevens to start the process of legalizing his status as Faith's father. He wasn't surprised to see Maggie, because of the joint scheduled meeting. But he wished he had a dollar for every time he saw her coming or going, when he wasn't expecting to. Bending to retrieve her daily newspaper and giving him a front row seat for viewing her cute, curvy backside. Or doing yard work she should have a man to do. Maybe he should offer. Maybe—

He shook his head. Thoughts like that one would get him in a world of trouble. From there it was a stone's throw to maybe they should be a traditional family—daughter, mother, father. And husband. He couldn't do that to Maggie. It was a fact that he was Faith's father and he planned to do the right thing by her. But he wouldn't compound anything by tying Maggie to him legally. He cared too much about her to do that.

If only he didn't have to see her all the time.

He turned back to lock his front door. There was a good possibility that a conspiracy existed against him, with his grandmother the brains, heart and soul behind it. Why else would she have made that ridiculous stipulation in her will? Had she known Faith was his daughter? Was Maggie telling the truth when she'd claimed that she'd told no one?

There. He'd done it again. His military training had taught him to look for the worst in people and he'd learned his lesson well. It was proof that he had no business acting on his feelings for Maggie. She deserved a man who saw light not darkness.

That was the reason he'd pushed her away the night before. It had cost him—big time. But it was the right thing to do.

She turned and he knew the exact moment she spotted him. Her whole body stiffened. In spite of the warm day, he felt a chill—from her.

He walked down his two steps and across his driveway to hers. "Hi."

She stood with her car door open. "Jack."

He saw pain followed by anger in her eyes. "Can I give you a lift into Destiny?"

"No, thanks. I have to open the shop when we're finished with Jensen and I'll need my car later." She lowered the sunglasses that were perched on her head.

"Okay."

Without another word, she got into her car and slammed the door. He watched her drive away. The cold shoulder was no more than he deserved after the way he'd treated her. The memory of kissing her sent shock waves of heat radiating through him even now. Everything about her was light and color, sunshine and sweetness. He craved her warmth like food, water and the air he breathed. He wouldn't change a thing about her. Which was why he would never push for an association past fathering Faith. It could change all three of them. And not in a good way.

A little while later Jack arrived in Destiny, just as Maggie disappeared inside Jensen's building. It was on Main Street nestled between the sheriff's office and Charlie's Tractor Supply, across from the urgent care clinic, This 'N That, and the computer store Maggie had told him about. He looked at the For Sale sign in the window for several moments, wondering if it was a sign in more ways than one.

Finally, he went inside for the appointment with his attorney. Jensen Stevens hadn't been there long, a fact that would have been obvious even to someone who wasn't detail-oriented. There was a desk in the center of the room with two folding chairs in front of it. Judging by the cords and wires on the floor, she had a working phone and computer. Maggie was already sitting.

"Hi, Jack," Jensen greeted him. "How are you?"

"Good," he lied. After that single word, silence echoed in the room. He felt as if he should make small talk. Unfortunately, his covert training hadn't prepared him to deal with an ex-lover who'd given birth to his daughter and the lawyer who was going to handle the details to make her legally his.

Jensen smiled. "Thanks for coming. This won't take long."

"Good. I have to get to work." Maggie didn't look

at him. She held herself as stiff as a military guard in front of the White House. Her hands were folded in her lap.

Jensen gestured, indicating he should take the other chair. "Sorry, this is all I have to offer at the moment."

"No problem." He didn't feel either woman needed to know that he'd spent days and weeks in places where there was no furniture at all or even a traditional roof over his head.

"This is all about paperwork," Jen said, looking from him to Maggie. "The first step is adding Jack's name to Faith's birth certificate. I'll file the papers with the county then petition the court to legally change her name to Faith Elizabeth Riley."

"Has a nice ring to it," he commented with a grin. He couldn't suppress his pride at the sound of that.

"Yeah, it does," Jen agreed. "There will be a waiting period. Then we'll have to appear before the judge and it all becomes final and legal. Any questions?"

"What about joint custody?" he asked.

"That's up to Maggie."

The woman in question glanced at him then, her eyes turning the shade of hunter green that meant clouds dimmed her sunshine. Guilt and regret pricked him.

"I have no objection. Faith wants to spend time with her father and I think it's important that she does."

"Child support?" Jack asked.

Maggie's small, pointed chin lifted a fraction. "I don't need anything from you."

Jensen cleared her throat. "The court will require support, or joint custody will be denied. You might want to reconsider, Maggie."

She shook her head. "Nope. Faith and I have been

doing fine on our own. I don't want or need to go down that road."

Jack half turned toward her. "But, Maggie—"

"Jack, my mind is made up. Keep your money and—"

Jen held up her hands. "We don't have to decide that today. If it becomes necessary, we can always go before the judge to institute support."

"No court has to tell me it's right to support my daughter," Jack said. "Decide what's fair and we'll do it now. Legal and proper. Along with medical benefits and anything else she needs."

"No one can accuse you of being a deadbeat dad," Jen commented.

"Through no one's fault, I was," he said. "Not anymore."

"Okay. I'll take care of it," Jensen agreed. "Unless either of you can think of anything else, I think that about takes care of what we need to start the ball rolling."

"That was fast," he said.

Jensen laughed. "I said it would be."

"Yeah, but I didn't really believe you," he commented. There it was again, always looking for the worst.

"Law is a lot about research and filing paperwork," Jen explained.

Maggie stood. "I have to go. Thanks for everything, Jen."

"My pleasure."

Before Jack could stand and get to the door to open it for her, she was gone. "That woman is fast," he said wryly.

"That woman is in love with you."

Jack's head snapped around to look at the lawyer. Maggie in love with him? Elation spread through him—followed swiftly by a brutal reality check. No way would a woman like her fall for a guy like him.

"You've been breathing too much of that research book dust, counselor."

Jensen met his gaze with a shrewd, penetrating one of her own. "I think you're in love with her, too."

Jack laughed, a sound without humor. "You're way off base."

"I don't think so."

"Is this part of your legal service?" he asked.

"Nope. Gut feeling. I've learned never to discount it. My gut is telling me that you and Maggie started something ten years ago that's alive and well today. You're crazy about each other. And I'm throwing that in for free."

"For all the good it does me," he muttered.

"So it's true?"

"Whether it is or not," he hedged, "there's no way I'll act on my feelings."

"Why?"

"I won't stick Maggie with a guy like me."

"And what kind of guy is that?" Jensen folded her hands together and rested them on the desk.

"Not the kind of man a woman like Maggie deserves."

"But, Jack, you two share a daughter. Which, by the way, I have to tell you is a major surprise. I don't think anyone had a clue the two of you even knew each other."

"We had to meet secretly. Because her parents didn't

approve of me. I don't think they knew how right they were." He ran a hand through his hair.

"That was ten years ago. You've both grown up. You share a daughter. You're going to interact. Judging by the sparks I saw, it won't take much more than that to ignite things again between the two of you."

"You're wrong. I'm Faith's father. I'm here to protect her legally, with my name. What's mine will go to her someday."

"Yeah. And emotionally?"

"I won't turn my back. I'll be around in a support capacity if she wants me. She'll never have to search for me. I don't want her to wind up on a talk show episode—'Kids Abandoned by Their Father.'"

Jen smiled sympathetically. "Instead you'll be in the episode titled—'The Woman Who Had My Child and Still Got Away.'"

"I'm not worth it."

"Don't you think that should be her decision?"

"I've done things, Jen. Things you don't talk about at the Fourth of July picnic, or the V.F.W. dance on Saturday night."

"You're one of those vets who served his country. You're one of the good guys."

"I've learned to trust my gut, too. And that's not what it's telling me. Sounds like another bad talk show."

Jen shook her head. "I'm starting to worry about you, Jack. Next thing I know you'll start reeling off the plots of daytime soap operas. You need to get a life."

"Takes one to know one. You're alone, too," he said pointedly. "Although I saw you and Grady at the rodeo, the night I got back into town. That has potential, counselor."

"If you're talking love life, you couldn't be further from the truth. That's not in the cards for me," she declared, her tone adding an exclamation point.

"Zach's been gone a long time," he said, gentling his voice.

"That's not what this is about."

He stared at her. "Then what is it about? I can't believe a knockout like you hasn't had opportunities—"

"Down, Jack. I had my chance. We're fixing you right now."

"I don't want to talk about Maggie."

"Understood. But if you're going to stay in Destiny, you need something to do."

"Yeah. I've been giving that some thought." He rubbed a hand across the back of his neck. "I noticed the computer store across the street is still for sale. I was thinking it might have some possibilities."

"I heard you're a whiz on the computer."

"That's the rumor. It's one of the things I trained for in the army." He leaned forward. "It might pay in the private sector."

"I don't see why not." She looked ruefully at the tangle of wires on her own floor that led to her computer. "I managed to plug everything in and get it working, but this isn't close to what I need. If you'd set up a system for me, I'd be eternally grateful. You can bill me for the time."

"You got it."

"I'll bet there are lots of businesses that could use your expertise. I can't be the only one who doesn't speak computer. It's geek to me."

"I just need a base of operations," he said, glancing over his shoulder to the store across the street.

"I could handle negotiations for you," she offered. "If you'll set up my computer system for me."

"It's a deal. Thanks, Jen."

She looked past him, through the window. "Here comes trouble."

He half turned in his chair to follow her gaze and saw the sheriff walk past the window. "Interesting phrasing. If I didn't know better, I'd say—"

"Don't go there, big guy," she warned. "You don't look a thing like Cupid. Grady and I would not appreciate you meddling."

"Okay." He stood. "I have to go."

"What's your hurry?"

"I've got to talk to Grady."

"I thought you were warned to steer clear of matchmaking."

He grinned. "Since when is everything about you? There's something I need to discuss with him and believe it or not, it hasn't got a thing to do with your love life."

One corner of her mouth lifted in a wry half smile. "Okay. Then you're dismissed."

"Thanks for the legal counsel." He headed for the door.

"But not the romantic advice?" she asked.

"On that note, I'll say goodbye," he said. "See you."

"Later," she answered.

He left her and went outside. "Grady," he called, increasing his stride to catch up with the other man.

The sheriff turned. "Hey." He walked back, stopping in front of Destiny's newest law firm. "You're just the man I was looking for. I saw you and Maggie go into

Jensen's office. One of my deputies said they'd seen her leave so I thought you had too."

She left, all right, Jack thought. Left him in the dust. "Jen and I were talking."

"Oh?"

He studied his friend. There was an edge to his voice, sharp as a hunting knife. He'd bet his last computer chip that Grady O'Connor was jealous.

"Yeah. We were discussing her love life."

"Is that so?" The words sliced the air between them.

"That's so," Jack said, struggling to hide a grin. "She's hot enough to melt butter, Sheriff."

"What's that supposed to mean?" Grady looked like a green sky about to spit out a tornado.

"Nothing. Just an observation."

"Better be."

"If I didn't know better, I'd believe you were jealous."

Grady leaned a shoulder against the post supporting the overhang. "She's just a friend."

"If you say so."

"Look, Jack, I've got problems and she's a distraction I don't need right now. We have to talk. Got a minute?"

"Yeah. I've been looking for information on Billy Bob Adams."

"You read my mind." Grady frowned. "Got anything yet?"

"'Fraid not. Everything I turned up made him look like a Boy Scout. But as I recall, he was in trouble as a kid."

"His folks always covered for him. Those records were probably sealed."

"Yeah. But that doesn't mean there's nothing recent," Jack pointed out.

"What's your plan?"

"I want to scan his picture onto some Internet law enforcement sites. Could turn up an alias."

Grady nodded. "That occurred to me, too. Can you do it?"

Worry carved deep lines into the sheriff's face. The man was facing the loss of his twin daughters unless Jack could come up with something that would help. The thought of two innocent girls in the slimy hands of anyone named Adams turned his blood cold. If someone tried to take Faith from him, he would move heaven and earth to stop it.

"Of course I can," Jack assured him.

"He's a user, Jack." Grady ran a hand across the back of his neck. "I feel it in my bones. He's just like his brother."

"My instincts are telling me the same thing. If we're right, he's left a trail."

Grady nodded. "A leopard doesn't change his spots."

He was proof of that, Jack thought grimly. "I'll do everything I can," he promised.

"Let me know if you find anything."

"You'll be the first."

"Thanks. Catch you later. I've got to run."

"I can't buy you a cup of coffee?"

"Some of us have gainful employment." The tension in him eased a bit. "I've got work to do."

"Some of us are fixing to find work," Jack countered.

"It's about damn time. Otherwise I'd have to run you in for vagrancy. See you later," he said, grinning. Then he disappeared inside his office.

Convenient that he and Jensen worked side by side, Jack thought. Maybe that boded well. Maybe the two of them could share something personal, something more than the wall between the spaces where they worked.

Jack glanced across the street to Maggie's shop. He sighed as regret, anger and pain twisted together and settled like a rock in his gut. He thought about Grady, facing the loss of his children. The bond he was developing with Faith. He'd only just found out about her, but his feelings were so deep he couldn't see the other side. While he had breath in his body, no harm would come to her.

Or Maggie, either. All these years she'd kept Faith a secret, protecting their child—protecting him. Yearning gathered inside him, so thick it pressed on his chest, nearly cutting off his air. If only he could be the kind of man Maggie deserved—a forever-after-till-death-do-us-part kind of guy.

But he wasn't. And he'd caused her enough pain. Now it was his turn to protect her. By pretending he didn't care. If it was the last thing he ever did, he would make sure his heart got that message.

Chapter 11

While Faith was at baseball practice, Maggie washed lettuce for their dinner salad. When she shut off the water, she heard an odd sound, like a watermelon going splat. Over and over again. She walked to the open door and realized the noise was coming from the backyard next door.

Jack.

The last time she'd seen him was earlier that day at Jensen's. Actually, that wasn't exactly the truth. She'd opened the shop, then kept her eye on the lawyer's office, counting the minutes he lingered with the stunning attorney. Jealousy was such an ugly thing and she hated to admit to it. But Maggie finally had to face the fact that she'd been green with envy—from celery to hunter and every shade in between.

Jack hadn't emerged from Jensen Stevens's office until Grady O'Connor had passed by and the two men had talked for several minutes. A pretty intense conversation if their body language was anything to go by. Then she'd seen Jack get in his car and drive out of town. She hadn't seen him since that morning.

Thump, thump, thump.

It sounded like he was hitting something. Maybe it was curiosity or just an overwhelming urge to see him, but Maggie let herself out the sliding screened door and peeked through the slat in the shared fence. The "aha" light went on when she saw the punching bag suspended from the sturdy frame of his patio cover. He was wearing a white T-shirt and gray sweat shorts. She sighed and hated herself for it.

Earlier that day in Jensen's office, she'd hardly said two words to him. She hadn't been able to let go of her anger at his pushing her away. It was a mystery to her how he could kiss her breathless and make her toes curl, then act as if nothing had happened. She'd sworn he was turned on, too. And she didn't think he was that good an actor. By God, she wanted an explanation.

And she wanted it now.

Afraid she would lose her resolve or give him too much of a heads-up if she took the longer route through her gate and then his, she climbed the tree. She shimmied across the limb on her backside before turning to her tummy to let herself down. Her exertions escalated her breathing and drowned out sounds, which accounted for why she didn't hear him approach. Without warning his hands were at her waist, lifting her effortlessly to the ground.

She turned to face him. "I have a bone to pick with you, buster."

"Okay."

When he brushed his arm across the sweat on his forehead, Maggie noticed his red knuckles, some of them scraped.

"New toy?" she said, lifting her chin in the direction of the punching bag.

He glanced over his shoulder. "A stress reliever. Every guy should have one."

"What about women?"

His gaze narrowed on her. "Why do I have the feeling that's a loaded question?"

"I really couldn't say."

"If I answer yes, you'll accuse me of something that I can't even guess. If I say no, you'll give me the women-are-as-capable-as-men speech."

She folded her arms beneath her breasts as she struggled to suppress a smile. The last thing she wanted to do was smile. Earlier, she'd been mad enough to spit nails. Now she was fighting to maintain the momentum. If she couldn't protect herself with anger, there was nowhere left to hide.

"Women are more capable than men. There's a reason the West wasn't settled until women got here. You might be bigger and stronger—"

Why did she pick that moment to zero in on his broad chest and muscled arms that would make a dyed-in-the-wool manhater whimper? Another telltale sigh welled up inside her and she barely managed to push it away, taking great satisfaction from her new mind-over-masculinity resolve.

"Go on," he urged, not bothering to hide his own satisfied smile.

"What?"

"Bigger and stronger?"

"Oh. That's a no-brainer," she said, reaching out to do the squeeze test on his rock-hard biceps. She swallowed—hard. "Guys *are* stronger. But women have everything else going for them."

"You won't get any argument from me about that."

His gaze moved over her from the top of her head, down her cropped yellow tank top and matching shorts, to her bare legs and feet. A gleam slid into his blue eyes. Somehow she knew he'd tried to suppress it and couldn't. So, she wasn't completely off base. She would bet everything she owned that he was attracted to her, too. So why had he pretended otherwise? She was going to find out, or break her heart trying.

"Did you climb over the fence just to insult me or was there something specific on your mind?" he asked, as if reading her thoughts.

"Actually there is something."

"Shoot." Still in the shade of the branches, he folded his arms over his chest and leaned back against the fence to listen.

She let out a long breath as she grappled with the thoughts tumbling through her mind, trying to bring some rational order to them.

"Any time today would be good, Mags."

She met his gaze and put her hands on her hips. "Okay. I was trying to think of a way to sugarcoat this, but I'll give it to you straight."

"I wouldn't have it any other way."

"Don't make fun of me, Jack."

"Perish the thought."

"Why did you get my motor running when you had no intention of stepping on the gas?"

He blinked. "You want to translate that for me, Magpie?"

"I think it's pretty clear. Last night—"

"What?"

"You kissed me as if you really and truly meant it. You wanted me. Then with no more explanation than—and I quote—'It won't work,' you walked away. What's that about, Jack?"

Instantly his laid-back manner disappeared. He straightened away from the fence and walked to the patio, stopping beside the punching bag.

She followed. Her cheeks were hot with humiliation, but she'd started this and retreat was no longer an option. "You might as well answer me, Jack. I'm not going away until I get an explanation. I'll wait you out. Redheads have a reputation for temper. But our stubborn perseverance is a well-guarded secret. So spill."

He spun toward her, his eyes bleak. "Okay. It's like this. I liked kissing you. I want you. Probably more than you'll ever know."

Her heart soared at his words. "So what's the problem?"

"I'm no good for you."

She shook her head. "Who died and put you in charge of unilateral decisions?"

"Damn it's hot," he said, grabbing the bottom of his T-shirt. "Don't make this harder than it already is."

"Why not? I want to make it as hard on you as possible. I think you should know—"

As she'd been talking, he pulled his shirt off and she was speechless. It wasn't the impressive expanse of chest covered with a masculine dusting of hair that silenced her. It was the scars. Several of them. The long, thin red line on his abdomen, just above the waistband of his shorts, had been a knife wound she guessed. Another wide mark on his shoulder might have been the path of a bullet that winged him. But the circular discoloration way too close to his heart stole the breath from her lungs and made her palms sweat. Fear, for what he'd gone through, for how close he'd come to dying, was a bitter taste in her mouth.

She moved close to him and traced the crescent-shaped scar. "Oh, Jack," she whispered.

He gripped her wrist and held her hand just a fraction of an inch from his flesh. "No pity. Not from you."

"It's not that—"

"You're wrong. That's all it can ever be." He dropped her hand as if it had burned him.

"Why?"

"We're too different, Maggie."

"Last night I, for one, was grateful for the differences. You're a man, I'm a woman. The rest is chemistry."

"It's got nothing to do with chemistry," he said roughly, glancing down at the mark on his chest.

"I think I'm as qualified as you to be the judge of that."

"You've got stars in your eyes. You still believe in fantasies, a happy ending."

"Why shouldn't I?" When he didn't respond, she protested, "I'm not what you think I am. I've got flaws and weaknesses. You said it yourself—a redhead's temper is legendary."

He shook his head. "You're sunshine and rainbows. I'm not."

A harsh laugh, just this side of hysterical, burst from her throat. She fought down the urge to give in to it. "If

I was bigger, I would shake some sense into you. I'd shake you until your teeth rattled."

"I've killed people."

That stopped her. She'd never known anyone who'd taken a life. "In self-defense. To save others."

"Not always. That would be too black-and-white. I live in the gray area. I've seen things—whole villages wiped out. Women and children massacred. You can't see things like that, do things that I've done, without paying a price."

"Besides protect yourself, what have you done that was so bad?"

Pain jumped into his eyes. That and the muscle contracting in his jaw were the only signs that he'd heard her. "I didn't protect the men in my charge."

"What do you—"

"It was a training exercise. My job was to make sure nothing went wrong. I planned, gathered information, prepared down to the smallest detail. I left nothing to chance."

"Jack, I don't—"

Intensity burned in his eyes—bright and hot. "There was an explosion, Maggie. A man died. Two others were hurt."

"How long ago?"

He rubbed the back of his neck. "Just before my grandmother died."

"It was an accident. War. A fact of military life."

"No." He shook his head. "There are missions where you expect casualties and you make the decision whether or not the objective is worth acceptable risk. This was a *training* exercise. No one was supposed to get hurt. But someone died and I didn't see it coming."

"You can't blame yourself."

"Then who? I was in charge. I should have seen something—done something to prevent it." He laughed bitterly. "Ironic, isn't it? I was a screwed-up teenage rebel your parents wouldn't let through the front door. In boot camp, I found something I was good at. I served my country and they would probably shake my hand, maybe even call me a hero. They might think I was good enough for you now."

"You are."

"No, I—"

She pointed at him, interrupting the protest. "I'm on a roll and would appreciate it if you wouldn't interfere with it."

"Okay." She noticed that one corner of his mouth quirked up. That was something, anyway. Maybe she could get through to him.

"You're the man who plucked my child from the jaws of death in the stock pen, with complete disregard for your own safety. And that was before you knew she was your daughter, too. You're a man, Jack, a brave man. You put your pants on one leg at a time and do the very best you can. But you're not perfect. Sometimes things happen that are out of your control."

He didn't answer, just let out a long breath and stared at a point over her head.

She reached up and framed his face with her hands, forcing him to look at her. "You need to focus on the things that are in your control. Like Faith. You took legal steps to adopt that little girl because it's the right thing to do. You resigned your commission to stick around for her."

He met her gaze then. “Did my grandmother know that Faith was my child?”

“No. Why?”

“Because you told me you hadn’t said anything to anyone. I’m convinced Gran put that wacky provision in her will to keep me here—because she knew. You didn’t tell her?”

“No.”

“What if I don’t believe you?”

“Come on, Jack. I agree that Dottie probably knew about Faith. But she guessed. She didn’t hear it from me. And she was a hopeless romantic who believed in happy endings. She threw us together and hoped nature would take its course. And she was right if last night was anything to go by.”

“You expect me to believe you didn’t even tell your parents?”

Maggie sucked in a breath against the pain of his words. Struggling to keep her voice calm, she said, “I never told anyone. God knows why, but from the moment I found out I was pregnant, it seemed important to protect you. My mom used to ask if Faith looked like *him.* All I said was yes. I finally told them her father was just a guy who wasn’t coming back. Just a guy who didn’t want me.” She shook her head. “Eventually, they just stopped asking questions. That’s the truth, Jack. If you don’t believe me, ask my folks.”

“That’s not the point. I just proved I’m a cynical bastard.”

He was another casualty of that training exercise fiasco, except his wounds were on the inside. He was willing to turn his back on happiness because he didn’t believe he deserved it.

"You're throwing up roadblocks. There isn't any couple who doesn't have doubts at one time or another. But we have to take a chance. It's called a leap of faith."

"Don't you get it, Maggie? That's what I'm trying to tell you. I don't have faith."

"Yes, you do. She's our daughter."

"Yeah, I—"

The squeak of the gate interrupted his response and they both looked there to see the daughter in question come into the backyard. Without noticing them, Faith quietly latched the gate. She turned and stopped short when she saw both of them staring at her.

"Why aren't you at baseball practice? Did it end early?" Maggie asked, her mother's instincts screeching that something wasn't right.

The child shrugged. "No. I was hot."

Maggie studied her daughter. "Were Stacey and Kasey O'Connor hot, too?"

"I dunno. Why?"

"Because I don't think Sheriff O'Connor made a special trip to camp just to drive you home."

"What does that mean, Mom?"

"It means that we agreed to carpool. I dropped the three of you off and he was supposed to drive you home when it was over."

"Oh."

"Yeah. Oh." She walked over to the girl. "How did you get home?"

"I walked," she answered, her head lowered.

"Faith Elizabeth Benson." She looked at Jack and said, "I mean, Riley. What were you thinking? I made arrangements for a ride so you wouldn't have to do that.

I don't want you alone on the street. And the sheriff will have a fit when he can't find you." She thought for a second and realized there were a number of pressing questions. "How did you know I was here?"

"I didn't," the girl said.

"Is our front door locked?"

"No," she said, shaking her head.

"Then I don't understand. Why did you come here?"

"I wanted to talk to my dad."

Maggie felt a tug in the region of her heart. "I see. You want to take it from here, Jack?"

Jack looked from mother to daughter and wished for a nice, simple covert mission. He'd never felt more out of his element. "What's going on, Faith?"

"It's all your fault."

The hair at his nape prickled. It was the same feeling he got when he sensed danger. The sensation was responsible for saving his life more than once. But the drop-dead look in his daughter's eyes told him his lucky streak had just run out.

"What's my fault?" he asked, his tone a cool, calm credit to all his training.

"They threw me out of baseball. I'm suspended. From the first game—maybe more."

"Why?"

"I'm the fastest one on the team, Dad. I'm the best batter. No one else can hit like I do. What if we can't get a run? What if we lose?"

"I asked you a question, Faith. Why did they suspend you?"

"He had it coming," she said angrily.

He let out a long breath and wondered if the circuitous route to the truth was a hereditary trait she'd inherited from her mother. He glanced at Maggie. Her expression swung from worried to irritated and back again. He took small satisfaction from the fact that she was as confused as he was. And he felt the most insane urge to pull Maggie into his arms and hang on for dear life. Because right now he had a nine-year-old who was up to her cute, shiny black curls in trouble. So far all he knew was that it was his fault and the boy had had it coming.

"What did you do?" he asked patiently.

"Gosh darn Logan Peterson." She started pacing, then walked to the patio and threw herself into one of the padded chairs. "He's such a dork."

"Why?"

"He's always bugging me."

Jack had wanted to take care of the little creep, but Maggie had stopped him. She'd urged him to let Faith deal with her own problems. What kind of solution had gotten her bounced from camp?

"Did you say anything to the adults around so they could handle it?" he asked.

"No."

"Care to explain why?"

Her small hands curled into fists. "I just got so mad."

"Faith, you need to give us all the facts," Maggie urged.

The child looked at her, anger and misery swirling in her blue eyes. "He was callin' me names, like he always does. I told him to quit it. My dad wouldn't like him messing with me."

"You're right about that," he said grimly. "I think I'll go talk to the little turkey—"

"Jack," Maggie said. "You need to get all the information before you do anything," she advised again.

"Okay." He let out a long breath. "Then what happened, Faith?"

"He said something else." The child glanced at Maggie, then at the hands in her lap, fingers twisting together.

"About you?" he asked.

"No."

"About me?" he questioned, figuring he had it coming.

"No," she said again, glancing at Maggie.

"About your mom?" he asked gently.

Faith met his gaze then, eyes so like his own flashing fire. "He said my parents aren't married. He called her a bad name. His mom should wash his mouth out with soap. He's such a jerk."

"What did you do? Unless you tell us, we haven't got a clue how to help you."

"You helped enough," she said, springing from the chair. "I kicked him the way I saw you doing it. Then I hit him in the nose with the side of my hand. I saw you do that, too. His nose was bloody and he fell down and scraped his elbow. Then they threw me out." She looked down at her hands. "I can't go back—not until Mom talks to them."

Jack felt as if he'd been kicked in the chest. She'd copied his moves? She'd decked the little creep? He was torn between pride and horror. Horror won when he realized she was right. It *was* all his fault.

If she'd never seen him practicing martial arts, she

wouldn't be in this fix now. He should never have come back. More important, he should have left. He would have—except for two things. Faith was his child and he wanted to be there for her.

And he was in love with Maggie.

Maggie walked over to the chair where their daughter slouched. "That's enough, Faith. You shouldn't talk to your father that way."

"Why not? It *is* his fault."

"He's not the one who kicked Logan Peterson then gave him a bloody nose."

Jack could have sworn he heard the smallest trace of amusement in her tone. She just didn't understand because she wasn't responsible for this mess.

"You guys don't understand—"

"Maybe not. But you need to go home and cool off, young lady," she said. "I'll be there in a few minutes. I need to talk to your father and we'll decide what to do with you."

"Yes'm." Faith stood and started for the gate, then turned. "I guess there's going to be something worse than dire consequences this time, huh?"

"We'll figure it out. Go," Maggie said, pointing.

When the child was gone, Maggie looked at him. "What's wrong? Are you planning to take on the nine-year-old boy who got your daughter in trouble?"

"That was the furthest thing from my mind."

"Not mine," she said. "I'd like to take the twerp out myself. I figured I'd have to hold *you* back. You're the family warrior."

"A family can't have too many warriors," he answered grimly. "Aren't you upset?"

"Of course I am. But it goes with the territory." She

took a deep breath. "Well, I better go deal with Little Miss Drama Queen. Do want to join me?"

He shook his head. "I trust you to handle it right. You've done a great job with her so far. Without me," he added.

Maggie touched his arm and looked up at him, a sympathetic expression on her face. "This, too, shall pass, Jack. Trust me. If a child doesn't hate you at least once a day, you're not doing your job as a parent."

"Most parents don't teach their kids to take out their friends."

"You're a good father. I'm glad you'll be there for backup when I have to face the camp director." When he didn't respond, she said, "Jack?" There were questions in her eyes.

"She's waiting for you. Take it from a guy who knows—waiting is the worst part. Don't drag it out for her."

She started to walk through the gate that Faith had left open. "But—"

"Go, Maggie."

She nodded and disappeared, never hearing him whisper, "Before I can't let you go."

Chapter 12

Jack dropped his packed duffel bag beside the front door and took one long, last look at his grandmother's living room. After he said goodbye to Maggie, he was outta here. He turned and reached for the knob, but before he could turn it, there was a knock.

He flipped the switch for the porch light, then opened the door. "Maggie."

"Hey. I saw your lights still on. Is it too late?"

It had been too late for them from the moment they'd met ten years before. Emptiness as big as the state of Texas opened up inside him. Unable to look away, he drank in the sight of her. To memorize the exact shade of her red hair when the light shone on it. To imprint in his mind the color of her eyes and watch them change when she was happy, sad or angry. To never forget the way it felt to bask in the glow of her sunshine.

"I was just on my way to see you. Come in." He

stepped aside and when she passed in front of him, the scent of flowers drifted to him. His fingers curled into his palms, to keep from grabbing her and holding her to him. If he did that, he would never be able to let her go.

A sad expression stole over her face as she glanced around, then laid a hand on the blue-and-green plaid sofa. Throw pillows in a floral pattern of the same colors adorned each arm and the matching love seat. A chair and ottoman in the same material as the pillows sat at an angle, completing the grouping. "Your grandmother asked me to help her pick out this furniture. Not too long before she died."

"There are a lot of memories here. Good and bad."

"Yeah," she said with a last glance around before meeting his gaze. "So, why were you coming to see me?"

"How's Faith?" he asked.

"Asleep."

"Isn't it a little early?"

"She cried herself to sleep."

The words squeezed his heart, but reinforced his resolve. "Is she okay by herself?"

Maggie nodded and her curls danced around her face. She looked like she could use a hug, making it damn near impossible to keep his promise to not touch her.

"I left her a note so she would know where I was." She peeked out the window. "Her room is right there."

He nodded. "I just want you to know I'm sorry."

"That's what I came over to talk to you about. I called the camp director and we have a nine o'clock appointment with him tomorrow, to get her reinstated." She retreated several steps, backing into his duffel by the door.

She glanced down, then at him. The look she shot him was all angry, stubborn redhead.

"What's this?"

"My duffel."

"No kidding. Why is it out—" she touched it with the toe of her sandal "—and packed?"

"I'm leaving. I was on my way over to tell you and Faith goodbye."

She folded her arms over her chest. "Silly me. I thought when you made the effort to adopt your daughter and buy a computer business in town—"

"How did you know about that?"

"It's Destiny, remember? No one keeps a secret."

"You did," he reminded her.

"This isn't about me. I thought you planned to be a permanent part of your daughter's life."

"You don't understand."

"Explain it to me."

"I can't stand to see her hurting." He ran his hand through his hair. "She's my child—my little girl. Dads protect their little girls."

"Bingo," she said. "And it's a whole lot more efficient to do that if you're actually living in the same town."

He should have known she wouldn't make this easy on him. Maybe if she knew what he was feeling. "Maggie, the slightest shadow on that little face rips my guts out. This time I'm responsible for putting it there."

"Part of a parent's job is showing a child how to take responsibility for their actions. But you're carrying that to a new level, Jack."

"Violence is a part of me and it's rubbing off on Faith. She was imitating me," he growled, pointing a finger at himself. "How can I stay and hurt her over and over?"

"Painful lessons are part of life. They're going to happen to her no matter what."

"I can't stick around and contribute to it."

"How nice that you can walk in and out of her life at will." Her voice was so cold. "I didn't get a choice. I carried her for nine months and when she was born, I was the only one there to take care of her. Thank goodness, my folks were there to support me. I don't know what I would have done without them. I'm glad I didn't have to find out. But there was never a question in my mind about hanging in for the long haul."

"I'm sorry—"

"I don't want apologies." She looked at the ceiling and caught her full bottom lip between her teeth. Then she met his gaze again and he wanted to take cover. "Do you think this is the first time she's been in trouble?"

"She was fine until I showed up."

She laughed, but there was no humor in it. "Hardly. Unfortunately underneath those black curls and that angel face, she's got my redheaded temperament and your rebellious flair. Up till now you've seen Daddy's little angel. You just hit your first speed bump, Ace. Silly me. I thought I was going to have backup for the first time ever."

"I'm doing this for you—for her. It was my watch. She got hurt. I should have seen it coming and didn't. Don't you get it, Maggie? There's a pattern forming. I won't take a chance with Faith."

"This isn't the army and you're not in charge. You and I are in this together."

He shook his head. "I tried. It didn't work."

"You're running away again. I can't say that it's the second time, because in all fairness you didn't know about her when you left the first time. But you ran away—into the army."

She was dead-on about that. And now he knew why. Because he didn't want to care. When you cared about people, pain followed. He'd never wanted to hurt this bad. Now it was too late. He loved his daughter and Maggie.

Always Maggie.

She waited for him to say something. When he didn't, she took a deep breath. "She made a mistake, Jack, not you. She did imitate what she saw you doing. There's nothing wrong with learning self-defense. She needs you around to teach her discipline, to help her control the knowledge of how to take care of herself, to show her the lesson when stuff happens, to guide her."

"The blind leading the blind."

"You think I don't know how scary it is? You of all people should know that heroes are afraid. But they face the fear and go on in spite of it."

"It's better for her if I just go. Trust me," he said.

"Nope." She shook her head and again the curls swirled around her face. "No way. I was just starting to do that. But I get it now. At the first sign of trouble, you run up the white flag and head for the hills. You're a coward and you don't deserve either of us. Trusting you won't happen. Not again."

"You'll thank me one day. I'm not very good father material."

She straightened her shoulders and dropped her arms, her hands clenching into fists. "Do you think good fathers are born that way? Parenting is trial and error. Do you think I haven't made mistakes? You're copping out."

"I'm sorry you feel that way."

She shook her head. "Who'd have guessed? You put your life on the line for your country. I've seen the scars to prove it, and your country calls you a hero."

He flinched at her words. "You're the real hero."

"Not really. I just show up every day and do the best I can. Because I love her more than anyone else could. Except you." She sighed. "This isn't all about Faith, is it? It's about me."

"What are you talking about?"

"I know I'm not the same girl I was ten years ago. That girl risked everything to be with you. She broke the rules for the chance to be in your arms."

"It wasn't your fault. I'm to blame."

She let out a long breath. "If you can't care about me, have the decency to say so. I'll get over it. But don't run out on her because of me."

He studied her, the fierce expression on her face. She'd once called him the family warrior, but she should look in the mirror. She was fighting passionately. And she was so wrong. He'd never loved her more.

He ran a hand through his hair. "If I didn't care about both of you—so much—I wouldn't be doing this."

She let out a long breath. "If you really believe that, you don't know what it means to care."

"From the beginning, I warned you about me."

"Too bad I didn't listen. I'm sorry I fell in love with you ten years ago and I'm sorry I love you now. How dumb was that—to let you back in—"

"Maggie—" He reached out to her.

She backed away, then gave him a wide berth as she moved around him, closer to the front door.

"Maggie, wait—"

"Not ever again, Jack." She yanked open the door then met his gaze. "You can stay or go. I'll do my best to not care either way. But you'd better be sure you make the right decision because you won't get a chance to hurt either one of us again. I got over you once, and it was the hardest thing I ever did. I'll get over you again."

Then she was gone and she took the sunshine with her.

Early the next morning, Maggie hustled Faith out their front door to the car. Don't look next door. Don't look. Don't you dare look, she warned herself.

"Dad's car is gone," Faith commented.

The words were like a punch to the gut. Against her own advice, Maggie glanced at the driveway beside hers to see for herself and noted that his car was indeed gone. Silly her. She couldn't help hoping she'd hammered some sense into him last night. She'd gotten in the habit of hoping since Jack Riley had returned. But habits could be broken. Just like hearts, she thought, steeling herself against the pain.

He didn't believe he deserved happiness. Now he was gone, along with any hope she had of convincing him that he was no different from every less-than-perfect human being and was entitled to forgiveness. He was a good man. In spite of her resolve, pain got through and stole her breath.

"Get in, Faith. We're going to be late."

"I don't care."

"I do." *About Jack,* her heart cried.

Maggie covered her red-rimmed eyes with her sunglasses and drove to the day camp at Destiny's park. Dragging her daughter by the hand, she crossed the grounds to the recreation building and found her way to the director's office. Christy, the cute, blond, blue-eyed teenage summer employee sat at the desk outside it.

"Hey, Maggie."

"Christy, I'd like to see Mr. Scott."

Rick Scott was also a teacher at Faith's elementary school. During the summer he supervised the day-camp program to supplement his income.

"He's with someone at the moment. He'll be with you in a minute. If you and Faith would like to take a seat," she said, indicating two plastic-seated chairs lined up against the institutional-green wall.

"I made an appointment," she explained. "I have to get to work."

"I'm sorry. A parent showed up unexpectedly. Mr. Scott will see you as soon as he can."

Maggie glanced down at her daughter. "I guess we wait."

"Great." Faith dragged herself to the chairs and plopped herself into one.

Before Maggie could join her, the office door opened and the camp director stood sideways in the entrance, looking at someone she couldn't see. The man glanced in her direction and she cringed. But instead of the disapproving expression she'd expected, he smiled a big friendly grin. "Hey, Maggie. Sorry to keep you waiting."

"No problem. But I'd like to speak with you to get Faith reinstated so that I can go to work."

"Everything is settled," he said.

Maggie blinked at the man. "What?"

"All Faith has to do is apologize to Logan and all will be forgiven."

The girl in question bounced out of the chair and stood rebelliously beside her. "I'm not sorry. I won't say it to that dweeb," she declared hotly. "You wouldn't want me to lie, would you?"

Unfazed, Rick Scott moved forward and stared at her. "You and Logan are going to sit down and apologize to each other. You'll talk this out. With a mediator. Your father and I decided it was the best course of action."

Father? Maggie's gaze shot to the doorway where she saw Jack now filling up the entrance.

He looked at his daughter. "Rick is right, kiddo."

Rick? He'd just met the man and now they were on a first-name basis, Maggie fumed.

Jack's intense gaze skimmed over Maggie, then returned to the child. "We figured there were skirmishes on both sides and it's time for a diplomatic solution."

"I don't know what that means," Faith said stubbornly. "But if it means kissing up to Logan Peterson, forget it."

Jack moved to stand in front of her and went down on one knee to look her in the eyes. "Sometimes we have to do things we don't want to because it's hard. That's life. Get used to it," he said in a firm tone that allowed no dissension in the ranks.

"But Logan started it," Faith argued, beginning to weaken.

Jack nodded. "Okay. But you two are going to finish it together—with words this time."

Maggie stood in stunned silence watching him deal with the situation like a commander who handled mutiny in the troops every day.

He hadn't deserted. Her heart soared.

Mr. Scott looked at their daughter. "Come on, Faith.

Let's go find Logan and the three of us will work this out."

"Dad?" she pleaded, looking at Jack.

"March," he said. "Get it over with."

"O-okay."

The camp director disappeared with their daughter and Jack stood, right in front of her. "Hi."

"Hi, yourself." She swallowed the lump in her throat. "I have the most insane urge to say—this is so sudden."

"Nope. After we talked last night..." He let out a long breath. "Actually, you did most of the talking—"

"Jack, I—"

He held up a hand. "I did some soul searching. You were right. I don't deserve you and Faith. I grew up an army brat moving around. Leaving my friends every time hurt. Eventually I learned to keep people out because I knew I was moving on."

"You must have been very lonely."

He nodded. "Until I moved to Destiny. There was Gran. I made some friends—Mitch Rafferty, Dev Hart and Grady. Not to mention a spunky redhead who was ready, willing and able to go AWOL for me."

"That was ten years ago."

"But you've always been in my heart, Maggie." He rubbed the back of his neck. "Gran knew it. She fixed me good, so I couldn't run away."

"You could have. And Destiny's rock lovers would have been pretty happy."

"What about you?"

After what she'd said to him last night, there was nothing left to lose. "I'd have been pretty *un*happy."

He grinned. "When I came back to settle her estate,

I didn't know who I was anymore. I was looking for myself, my soul. I found you and Faith. Gran knew I was lost and she knew you were my destiny. She made sure I found both of you right next door."

"I wish I could thank her." Her heart started to pound like the bass drum in Destiny's Fourth of July parade.

"Yeah. And I have to thank you, too. Because I wanted to run. But you made me face up to my past. You showed me that I could forgive myself, that I was worthy of love. You were right about me. I am a coward."

"Oh, Jack—I didn't mean it. I was angry."

He shook his head. "No. You were dead-on. But I found I was more afraid of spending the rest of my life without you and our daughter than being a failure."

"Well, you sure handled *Rick,*" she said dryly.

The corners of his mouth turned up. "Last night, I almost came to you a thousand times to ask for another chance to do better. Then I realized words wouldn't cut it. Somehow, I had to show you I meant it. So I handled Rick. I plan to stay in Destiny for the long haul."

Maggie knew he was talking about their daughter. "Faith will be glad to hear that."

"What about you?"

"I'm glad you'll be staying for her."

"No, I mean how do you feel about you—and me?"

"I bared my soul last night." She met his gaze. "Now it's your turn. If you want."

"Oh, I want." The intensity in his gaze added power to the simple words. "I love you, Maggie. It's ten years late, but I mean it ten times more. I need you. Somehow I think you already know that." The expression in his blue eyes was so earnest it tugged at her heart. "If you haven't changed your mind about what you told me last night, I'd like to ask you to marry me."

"Okay."

"Okay I can ask? Or okay you will?"

"You can ask *and* I will. You're a good man, Jack Riley, and I plan to spend the rest of my life convincing you of that fact."

"Does that mean you still love me?"

She moved against him and wrapped her arms around his waist as she pressed her cheek to his heart. The pounding made her smile and she tightened her hold.

"Yes, I love you. It's always only been you. If you don't know by now—"

The tender kiss he placed on her lips showed her without words how he felt. Jack Riley was her past, present and future. Her destiny. She would love him forever and always. Ten years ago she'd known it. Now, finally, he believed it, too.

* * * * *